THE HAND OF ROBIN SQUIRES

Joan Clark

THE HAND
OF ROBIN SQUIRES

Illustrations by William Taylor and Mary Cserepy

CLARKE, IRWIN & COMPANY LIMITED   TORONTO   VANCOUVER

Canadian Cataloguing in Publication Data

Clark, Joan, 1934-
  The Hand of Robin Squires

ISBN 0-7720-1091-9

I. Title.

PS8555.L353H35   jC813'.5'4   C77-001272-8
PR9199.3.C53H35

© 1977 by Clarke, Irwin & Company Limited

ISBN 0-7720-1091-9

1 2 3 4 5 JD 81 80 79 78 77

Printed in Canada

To my mother and father

The author would like to thank the Canada Council
for providing funds to research this book.

THE HAND OF ROBIN SQUIRES

Before I begin, I must tell you that I am writing this story not only for you, but also for myself, for in telling my tale I am putting aside my old life and freeing myself for the new.

A new life awaits me across the ocean, of that I am sure. I have earned my passage, and as soon as the autumn hurricanes have blown past this port of Boston, I will go home to England, where my story began that fateful summer five years ago.

I was fourteen that summer, an age when mystery and adventure are more attractive than wisdom and caution. Even now, though I am older and surely wiser, I cannot keep my mind off that island. Memories of its deserted coves, thick fogs and swirling seagulls come back to me as sharp and clear as that day in 1704 when I first stepped onto its cursed shores. Believe me, that island is cursed; the many who can testify to that are dead. I am the only one who can set the matter straight. This I intend to do, for unless I tell my story, no one, no matter how clever he may be, will ever know what lies buried on that island.

1

Chapter One

To tell this story I should begin not in 1704 but the year before, in the early spring of 1703. My father and I were working in one of the back sheds of my grandfather's manor house in Shilston, England. My grandfather was, as his name and ours suggests, a squire. Though he owned many acres of farming land, he did not farm them himself. Being old and crippled, he spent most of his time bundled up in blankets beside the kitchen fire. Sometimes, if the day was particularly warm, he would hobble out past the barns to stare rheumy-eyed across the line of fields broken only by green copses pocketed neatly in the small valley where the stream ran. He was not afoot on this particular day, which I remember was one of those bitter cold damp spring days that makes feet ache and noses drip. It was a day certain to aggravate my grandfather's gout.

Nevertheless his tenant farmers were about, plough-ing the rich dark earth, readying it for early corn even though a thin crust of brown ice still edged the field on the north side. There were three men ploughing, breaths steaming, hands wrapped in flannel against the cold. Occasionally they stopped to drink from a jug of corn whiskey: their winter's work and one of their few pleasures. Even though they were desperately poor, dependent entirely on my grandfather's whims for their livelihood, there were smiles on their faces as they talked together and licked up the whiskey that dribbled off their stubbled chins.

"Do you intend to hold this valve open for me? Or would you rather push the plough?" my father asked impatiently.

I turned to help him.

My father was slow to anger but I must admit my daydreaming did sometimes irritate him, especially when he needed an extra hand with a tricky length of pipe or a bolt.

"I was just thinking how happy those peasants are," I murmured. "They are so poor. What have they got to be happy about?"

My father put down his wrench and looked me squarely in the eye. "They are happy because they have nothing. Wealth, possessions, goods, all these things are responsibilities," he said slowly. "The more you possess the more you must concern yourself about making it secure. Not having any money has one big advantage. You don't have to worry about keeping it."

"Yes, but somebody has to have money. We have to have food and shelter and clothing!" I spoke with such earnestness that my father laughed.

"You sound like your grandfather," he chided.

"I didn't intend to!" I protested and felt my cheeks grow red.

Unwittingly I had taken my grandfather's point of view, which was opposite to my father's. For years I had heard my grandfather harangue my father about money, or rather, his lack of it. Yet I had never really thought about it until now. My father had absolutely no interest in money and as far as I know, never earned any. As my grandfather reminded him, this was possible only because he housed, fed and clothed both of us. This situation did not seem to bother my father but it sometimes made me feel awkward and useless. I yearned for the day when I could support myself without my grandfather's help.

Had my father and I taken over the farm, it might have been different. My grandfather wanted one of his sons to manage his squiredom. He had only two sons: Edward, who had gone off to sea at fourteen, and my father, Charles, who had no interest in farming. Consequently a day did not pass without my grandfather bringing up the subject of who would manage his estate when he was gone. It became increasingly evident that since he considered my father a failure, it had to be me. I have to admit that I was not interested in becoming a squire either. I was far more intrigued by my father's work.

In spite of the fact that my father did not do farm chores, he was never idle and worked far more diligently than anyone I knew. Right now, though not mending the plough or milking a cow in one of the many sheds built helter-skelter across grandfather's yard, we were working hard. Or at least my father was. One does not invent a pump in a matter of days. It takes years of designing, experimenting and fitting together.

"Another day or two," he said, "and we should have it ready for the mine."

Several of his pumps had been tested at a mine in Cornwall where underground water was a continual hazard to the miners. They had proved partly successful,

5

lifting the water some ten feet, and thrusting it upwards to forty feet. But my father knew he could do better than that. Working on what he had learned in those tests, he had modified the pump so that it could thrust the water to much greater heights. All winter he had been redesigning and forging new parts in his smithy. Now the pump was nearly ready.

I was enormously proud of my father and was looking forward to the trip to Cornwall. I visualized us loading the pump onto one of my grandfather's wagons and riding the bumpy rutted roads to the mine. There the miners would stand around the edge of the open pit, staring wide-eyed as my father checked the platforms built every ten feet into the shaft. When he was satisfied they were adequately shored up to support the weight of the pump, he would set up the pulley and begin lowering the parts into the hole where they would be assembled. For centuries the miners and their ancestors had been sloshing through underground water, often being put out of work by it. Now all this was about to be changed by my father's ingenious engineering feat.

I think he deserved whatever admiration he got, for he was a genius. Had he lived, it would have been just a matter of time before his fame spread across Europe. His discoveries would have been patented, and he would have become a member of the Royal Society, a group of highly esteemed scientists and inventors.

On that cold spring day when my father and I were working on the pump in the back shed, these daydreams were interrupted by the gallop of horses. As the thundering hooves clearly signalled that their destination was our manor, I ran outside to see who it could be, then immediately ran back in shouting, "FATHER! COME QUICKLY! IT'S UNCLE!"

Uncharacteristically, my father dropped what he was

6

doing and ran into the courtyard to meet Edward, his older brother, resplendent in black velvet and white lace, come home from the sea after an absence of two years.

Chapter Two

Edward sat handsome and tall on a white gelding. He was, as usual, clean-shaven, his moustache neatly trimmed, his black hair tied back at the nape of his neck. He wore no wig. When ashore my uncle liked wearing the latest fashion, and he cut a fine figure in whatever outfit he chose. In this respect, as in most others, he was totally unlike my father, who never gave his appearance a second thought.

There were two men with my uncle, both sitting astride a single black mare. They had with them a chestnut stallion, saddled but riderless. One of the men on the black mare was a barrel-shaped red-haired giant of a man with hands as rough and raw as chunks of meat. Although he was dressed in an expensive, tailored suit, he looked like he more properly belonged in coarse serge than in fine linen. No tailor's skill could offset the untidy beard which grew from his chin in irregular tufts like clumps of red weeds. Nor could the lace collar soften the

hardened, heavy-featured face, scarred as a battle-ground.

His companion was even more unusual. He resembled a monkey more than a man, clinging to the big man's back like one of those long-armed jungle creatures. His domed head was bald except for a few wispy hairs that grew round his small protruding ears. His brown eyes, set well back in a wrinkled brow, watched us unblinkingly. What a strange trio these three men made!

My father was the first one to reach my uncle's side. Edward slid his long legs to the ground and they shook hands perfunctorily. It could not be said that the two brothers were close or even good friends. There was a six year age difference between them: my father was eight when Edward went off to sea. And of course Edward had not been back for anything but short visits since. When these visits did occur, it became evident how very different the two brothers were: the one a successful naval captain who had spent most of his adult life at sea and the other an inventor who was content to spend his life experimenting in the rural countryside of England. Each time the two brothers met, the gulf between them widened and they shook hands across it, exchanged a few polite inquiries and then retreated, each into his own domain. This visit, however, was to be different from all the others.

There was about my uncle an impatience, an eagerness I had never seen in him before. His visits were usually light and casual. He came bearing expensive and exotic gifts which he carelessly distributed among us. These gifts always impressed me and my grandfather as well, though I could never admit my pleasure because my grandfather always took this opportunity to remind my father that he never gave any such gifts.

There were no gifts this time. As soon as my uncle had shaken hands, he drew my father aside. Though he spoke in a low voice, I heard him say, "Charles, I have an urgent matter I wish to take up with you."

I saw my father's eyebrows arch inquisitively: what could Edward want with him?

"It is a matter of utmost importance . . ." My uncle stopped in mid-sentence when he saw me. "Can this be Robin? How you've grown!" which was true. In the past two years I had already surpassed my father's short stature. Then my uncle added after a pause, "And what big ears you have!"

I took this sly comment in good spirit.

"The better to hear you with!" I retorted lightly.

My uncle's dark eyes assessed me briefly. Then he laughed. "Well now, and quick too."

"Too quick sometimes," my father remarked drily. Then he turned his attention toward the other two men. The big man had dismounted and was lifting the smaller one down. It was then that I noticed the "monkey" had no legs: they had both been severed above the knees.

"And who are these men?" my father inquired.

"The big one is Billy Boles, my first mate. The other is Powderlegs, ship's surgeon. Both have been my loyal shipmates for over ten years."

We watched as Billy Boles untied a pair of crutches that were strapped to the back of the horse. When he was hunched over his crutches, Powderlegs came scarcely up the bigger man's waist. The two approached us and exchanged civilities. Though the big man, Billy Boles, made an attempt to be friendly, it did not dispel my immediate distrust of him. It was not the gruff voice and blackened teeth that showed when he tried to smile, but an ominousness I could almost smell. It was more than the foul stench of his breath; it was an odour of evil that permeated him entirely. The other man, Powderlegs, was much as he looked: an alert, quick, friendly fellow, though not nearly so beguiling as he first seemed.

11

After the necessary introductions we went inside. My grandfather treated my uncle like the prodigal son come home. He ordered the fattest hog curing in the smokehouse to be cooked over the fire and set Annie, our cook and nurse since my mother died, to fetch some spiced wine.

Later in the evening after we had eaten, I was sent up to the garret to sleep. My uncle was to sleep in my room. Reluctantly I dragged my straw mattress up the ladder and lay down upon it. I could not sleep. I was not used to this airless, raftered room, but that was not the real reason. I knew that with me out of the way, my uncle and father would talk far into the morning. All during the evening my uncle had been restless. It was clear he was biding his time impatiently, tolerating the family feast until he could speak privately with his brother. What was it he wanted from my father?

Chapter Three

I slept late into the morning. When I finally stumbled into the kitchen for breakfast, only Annie and my grandfather were there. I had expected to see our guests sitting around the plank table, idling over breakfast. Annie shoved a bowl of lumpy gruel in front of me. Obviously it had been scraped from the bottom of the pot. I grimaced.

"That's all that's left, Robby boy. Them that comes tardy gets the leavings." Annie disliked stragglers and never failed to show it.

But I was too hungry to go without. Between mouthfuls I managed a question. "Where are the others?"

"They're in the stable with the horses. Your father's upstairs—packing."

"Packing!" I slammed down my spoon so hard my grandfather snapped from his reverie with a startled grunt.

"That's what he told me," Annie said matter-of-factly.

"He's going to Am-er-e-kay."

I raced upstairs. My father was at his desk sorting through papers. A saddlebag lay open on the floor and into it he had neatly stowed his books.

"Is it true we're going to America?" My voice was hoarse with excitement.

"Sit down, Robin," my father said quietly.

Only when I had dragged a stool out of the corner and sat down did my father turn around and face me, and even then he did not look me straight in the eye as he usually did, but kept glancing nervously at the papers in his lap. I had the impression he had prepared a speech beforehand and was now reluctant to give it.

"Well?" I prompted.

"Robin, this is hard for me to explain, but the fact is I've decided to go to America to do some work for Edward, and I'm afraid it's not possible for you to come."

I could not believe my ears, "You mean I can't go?"

"I'm sorry, but no, you can't."

"But why not?" My voice shook with the unfairness of his going off on an adventure without me and more important, with the horror of being separated from him. My father and I had never been apart. Our closeness was due in part to the fact that my mother had died when I was born and since I was his only child my father spent much of his time with me. As soon as I learned to read and write, he began explaining his theories and scientific experiments to me, mainly, I think, because there was no one else around to whom he could talk. The result of all this was that the bond between us was very strong.

"Robin, I have agreed to design and build something for Edward and I have promised him that I will not discuss the details with anyone—not even you. I can tell you though that it is an enormously challenging project which will require my fullest attention. Even if you were to come I would have no time for you."

14

I was about to assure him that I would find something to do on my own but he went on, "And there are your examinations. If you come with me now you would miss the goal we have been working towards for two years."

This was true. After my twelfth birthday I had begun concentrating on passing exams that would eventually qualify me to enter university. Because my grandfather considered education a waste of time, my father had never gone to university, but he was determined that I should go. He had sent me to a tutor for my Greek, Latin and French but all other subjects he had taught me himself, for although he had not attended university, he had taught himself a good deal. I was getting close to my goal of writing the examinations in the fall.

Nevertheless I blurted out, "But think what an education travel is!" Visions of America's new and untried lands loomed large in my mind: what could be more educational than discovering the undiscovered?

My father smiled at this. "True. But America will still be there when you've finished your studies."

"You mean I can go some other time?"

My father would not commit himself. "Possibly. Edward's project will require me to make two voyages to America: this trip when I will begin the project, and another next spring when I will complete it. Perhaps you will be able to accompany me then. Naturally I shall return home for the winter to work on the design and improve my pump's efficiency. In any case Edward tells me that work on the project will be impossible during the winter months since North American winters are always severe. So you see, I shall be back here in the autumn, and with your studies to occupy you while I'm gone, it will seem no time at all before I return. Now," my father concluded briskly, "help me pack."

I was given the task of packing his surveying instruments and then his clothes while he continued to sort

15

through his papers. By the time we had packed all his effects and carried them outside Edward and the others were waiting with the horses saddled. I knew now why my uncle had arrived yesterday with a riderless horse; it was because he intended to carry away my father today.

Their departure was swift. There was no time for prolonged good-byes. It was all I could do to watch my father leave. As they left the courtyard and galloped down the road, I felt like running after them but the thought of what a fool I would make of myself in front of my grandfather held me fast. I stood quietly beside the old man, feeling lonelier than I had ever felt before. I was aware of a dull ache inside my chest, an empty feeling, one that has never entirely left me.

It was not until the four travellers were out of sight that I had time to question the abruptness of my father's departure. How strange it was that all of a sudden he had decided to quit his native countryside which up to now he had shown no desire to leave. What was it that induced him to abandon his experiments, especially his new pump, and go to America?

Chapter Four

After my father left, I did not dig into my books as he had encouraged me to do. In fact months went by without my opening a notebook. I conveniently "forgot" my lessons with my tutor. Was it bad temper that made me behave so? Partly. After my father had gone, I became angry that he had not taken me and in defiance refused to have anything to do with my studies. I was not even sure I wanted to take my exams.

I went for long rambling walks over the greening countryside. I fished in our trout stream with the tenant farmers' sons, and went swimming where the water pooled deep and clear beneath the willow tree. For the fun of it I helped with the spring sowing and later with the hoeing. All this physical, non-bookish behaviour pleased my grandfather who, now that the weather was warm, frequently wandered out to the fields to oversee the work. I think he believed that now that I was away from my father's influence I would make a country squire after all.

But as summer lengthened into autumn and harvesting came, I grew bored with work in the fields and turned back to my studies. I knew that it was a matter of weeks before my father returned, expecting me to be more learned than I was.

Sometimes I took my books to the windowseat where I could study and watch the road at the same time. One day in late October my vigilance was rewarded. I saw my father far down the road, his horse laden with its burden of drawings and maps made in America. The horse could not move fast enough for me. Shouting joyously, I ran out of the house and down the road, reaching my father's arms long before his horse trotted into the courtyard.

My father looked thinner and more tired than I expected. I had imagined the voyage would have been more pleasurable than he indicated. He did not like sea travel, he said; it made him ill. But he was enthusiastic about what he had seen of North America. He had drawn many pictures of the shore of Acadie past which he had sailed. The sketches showed a rugged coastline broken by long wave-ridden beaches. He had also done many drawings of a large bay with countless islands. The islands were of many different shapes and sizes, some large and sprawling, others barely more than clumps of rock.

But he had no pictures of Indians which greatly disappointed me. In all my imaginings of North America, I had pictured meeting a race of red-skinned, dark-eyed people about whom I knew little except what I had learned from the accounts of explorers. My father saw no such Indians. They were there in great numbers, he said, but on the mainland itself. He had not been on the mainland but offshore on one particular island.

18

Except to tell me that the job he was doing for Edward was well underway, he would not discuss what took place on that island. It seemed to me that my father returned home a changed man. Whatever it was he was building absorbed him so totally that he behaved as though he were possessed. He did, however, help me with my studies. He said nothing about my summer's sloth, either because he understood the reasons for it or because he was too preoccupied to notice how far behind I had slipped. When he was not helping me, he worked far into the night. His eyes took on a peculiar overbright expression as if he were being driven by some unexplained unnatural force. He hardly touched the food Annie begrudgingly carried up to him because he so frequently failed to turn up at mealtimes. He also spent a good deal of time in the back shed with the pump. Only on these occasions did he allow me to interrupt my studies so that I could help him with some adjustment. Once he said to me, "Robin, this pump will be required to do a job at which it cannot afford to fail."

My exams in Dartmouth began just before Christmas. I worked long and hard and on the appointed day my father and I rode there over the frozen ground. For three days I sat in the cold, drafty room and wrote down everything I knew, while my father waited for me at the inn where we were staying. When the exams were over, we unwisely decided to return home that same day though it was well past noon. I am firmly convinced that had we stayed on in Dartmouth and rested, we might have been spared the tragedy that followed.

As it was, we rode straight into the season's first blizzard. It swept across the moors with unrelenting fury, the wind biting through our clothes, the snow sweeping across the road. The bitter cold numbed our hands as the snow beat against our heads. I begged my father to stop but he pressed on, driven by the same force that had

19

been driving him since he had returned from his voyage with Edward. It was late in the evening when we finally rode into the yard of my grandfather's manor. Fortunately Annie had kept lamps in the windows. So frozen were we that the sleepy groom had to lift us from our saddles. Annie had hot broth waiting which we drank, more grateful for its warmth than for its nourishment. I did not think I would ever be warm again and spent the night on the floor in front of the fire, in spite of having to listen to my grandfather's nocturnal groanings and snorings as he slept on his bed in the kitchen corner.

The next day my father took ill, developing such a high fever that no amount of wiping his forehead could keep it free of sweat. Annie and I did our best to nurse him until the day after, when I, too, fell ill. I do not remember much about the earlier part of my illness. Annie later told me that for over a week I was burning with fever, that I scared her out of her wits with my yells and disjointed ramblings; in my wild imaginings our house had become a wooden ark that wobbled as waves crashed around it while lions and tigers galloped around the room and across my bed, their heavy paws trampling my chest. As fearful as these delirious hallucinations were, they were far better than the reality that lay beyond them.

As soon as my fever broke and I was in control of my own mind again, Annie told me my father was dead.

Chapter Five

I shall not recount the details of the next few months: they were sad, dreary times. The combination of my father's death and my own illness robbed me of energy and enthusiasm. I spent those wintry days in the kitchen chair opposite my grandfather. Annie made me savory stews, my favourite pies and tarts to tempt my appetite but I ate little. I had absolutely no desire to go anywhere and sat around far longer than was needed for me to convalesce. I could not bear to visit my father's churchyard grave where he had been buried beside my mother. Even the news that I had passed my exams did not excite me; what did it matter now?

My melancholy was hard on Annie and my grandfather. They constantly conspired to get me going to divert me from grief. There were messages, most of little importance, to be delivered to the overseer. The stable was to be checked and rechecked: my grandfather had lost a horse to the cold the winter before and he did not want it to happen again. I was regularly posted at the front window upstairs to watch for traffic along the road. Increasingly my grandfather talked about the press-gang; they came through every year at winter's end, he said, though I did not remember seeing them the past year. It was true, however, that two years previously, one of his tenant farmer's sons had been clamped into chains and carried off to serve in Her Majesty's Navy. Even the fear he tried to instil that I, too, might be taken in such a manner did not lift me from my gloomy state. Nothing upset, touched or interested me—until Edward arrived. And then the change in me was instantaneous.

He came as before, in early spring. Only now he came in a coach and four, and, excepting a driver, alone. This time he was dressed in what I took to be a naval uniform cut from heavy blue wool with gold trim on the collar and gold buttons down the front. From my post in the same front window through which I had seen my father's return, I saw the coach coming along the road. When it pulled into our yard and my uncle stepped out, I ran down to the kitchen.

"It's Edward! He's come back!"

This startled my grandfather from his afternoon nap.

"Edward, you say? Good. Good. I've been waiting for him to show up."

Annie stopped her work and peered through the window. She did not seem to share our pleasure. Perhaps she sensed how he would react when he heard about his brother's death, or maybe it was simply that Edward's visits always meant more work for her.

As soon as he swept into the kitchen exchanging the usual brisk greetings, he looked around.

"Where's Charles? In his study, I suppose?"

The three of us: my grandfather, Annie and I looked at

one another. A lump grew in my throat and I could not say the words.

"He took a chill and died before Christmas," my grandfather said matter-of-factly. "The boy's been sick with it too. It's a wonder I didn't get it."

Edward stared at us in disbelief. "Surely this cannot be! Is this true?"

"It's true all right." Annie said.

Anger erupted in my uncle with all the violence of a volcano shooting out erratic bursts of fire.

"That cannot be! He cannot be dead. Cannot!" He paced the floor back and forth. "Why did he die? That was not part of our agreement. Why would he do such a thing?" He pounded the table so hard a plate bounced off and smashed on the floor. "I cannot accept this. The unfairness of it! Charles had no right to die!"

Though my father's death weighed so heavily on me that I preferred not to talk about it, my uncle's reaction was too unreasonable for me to remain silent.

"Do you think he wanted to die?" My voice shook with grief and anger. "You talk as if he had a choice. None of us wanted him to die and I'm sure he didn't either!" My uncle stopped his frantic pacing and looked at the tears spilling unashamedly down my cheeks.

"Ah yes," he said heavily, "I can see it is true. He really is dead. What he started he cannot finish." My uncle then gave a peculiar laugh, a dry, brittle sound. "The irony of it. Chance puts opportunity on board then poof! snatches it away. Just like that!"

He turned to me.

"His papers! Where are they?"

I shrugged.

"They're in his room," Annie said sullenly. I could see that she was annoyed by Edward's callous response to his brother's death. "I left everything the way it was."

24

My uncle turned abruptly and went upstairs. I followed, suddenly concerned about my father's belongings. His notes, his lifetime's work were in that room. Although I had not interested myself in them since his illness, it occurred to me that, as my father's nearest kin, his papers were rightfully mine. I kept close to Edward's heels. Ignoring me completely, he opened the door of my father's room and crossed to the desk. He leafed wordlessly through the papers there and then turned his attention to the shelves beside the desk. On three shelves were three stacks of papers, each with its own paperweight. He removed a paperweight and looked through one of the piles.

"These are what I'll need. Perhaps with some study on my part, I shall be able to finish it myself."

"Finish what?" I put in quickly.

Edward did not answer. He turned his attention to the other two piles. "And I shall need these. There is no question about it. Charles was very clever and very thorough, so much so that I might be able to manage without him." Whereupon he began to pick up the papers.

I stepped boldly in front of him, snatching the papers from his hands. He looked as if he was going to strike me. His eyes grew wild and angry. I stepped away from him hugging the papers close to my chest, suddenly fearing him, even though he was my uncle. This did not, however, prevent me from trying to protect my father's work. My uncle did not understand how much study and effort went into what he considered were nothing more than skillfully drawn designs.

"Aren't you forgetting, Uncle," I said, clearing my throat, "that these papers are rightfully mine? I inherit all of my father's possessions."

At the mention of the word "possessions," Edward's

face relaxed. His eyes lost their wild look. He actually laughed, perversely amused by my words.

"Well now, and what if I told you that your father and I had an agreement and that these papers are mine as part of that agreement?"

"Oh I know all about the agreement," I said loftily. Deliberately I hoped to indicate I knew more about their agreement than in fact I did. I knew I had to use bluff in dealing with my uncle. "But I do not think my father received payment for his part of the agreement."

His eyes narrowed. "Oh, so that's it. It's money you're after. I can see you are far more aware of the value of money than your father was. Very well, I shall give you a hundred pounds before I leave as my part of the agreement."

I swallowed hard. A hundred pounds! That was more money than I had ever seen. Still there was something I wanted more and, as so often happens, it wasn't until the words were out of my mouth that I realized how true they were.

"I want to go with you," I blurted out, "to America."

My uncle did not take me seriously. "Do you now!" he said. "And what possible use could you be to me there?"

This reaction I knew very well was calculated to make me feel that I could be no use at all. But I refused to plead with my uncle: I sensed that if I were to beg I would be ill-treated and ignored for my trouble. I have met people like him since; they respect only those who will stand up to them; everyone else is, by default, their inferior. So I replied as haughtily as I could, "I know how to use my father's surveying equipment and he often talked to me about his theories."

"Is that so?" my uncle sneered. It was clear that he did not believe me. Still clutching my father's papers, I retreated downstairs.

26

Presently my uncle appeared in the kitchen. My grandfather was waiting for him.

"Sit down, Edward. I want to talk to you."

Playing the role of the docile son he never was, and would never be, Edward sat in the chair opposite my grandfather.

I retreated to the shadows on the far side of the room.

"Now, Edward," my grandfather began, "I wish to speak to you plainly about the boy." He pointed a crippled finger toward me then leaned closer to Edward. "Take him to sea!"

I could scarcely believe I had heard properly. My grandfather sending me off to sea! I thought he would keep me here forever, if need be, to work his estate.

"It is what he needs," my grandfather spoke slowly. "Since Charles died he has done nothing but mope around. He needs a change. Take him. Put him to work. It will do him good." The old man's voice quavered. "Mark my words, if you don't take him, the pressgang will get him. What with Queen Anne's War dragging on and on, they'll be looking for every able-bodied male, be he man or boy, to work Her Majesty's ships. If they come here, I'll not be able to stop them. They took John Sewell's older boy and he couldn't do a thing about it there were so many of them. If the pressgang gets Robin, he'll become nothing more than a slave. If *you* take him, his chances are better."

My grandfather sat back in his chair exhausted by what was, for him, a long speech. Edward listened to all this with his long legs crossed, his elbows on his knees, hunched over, stroking his moustache in what appeared to be a thoughtful manner. But when my grandfather was finished his discourse, it was clear his words had not made the slightest difference to him.

27

"Father, I cannot take him. Not on this voyage. This one is to be different from all the others. Maybe next year when I've finished what I've set out to do, I will take him."

"But you are Charles' brother," the old voice croaked with indignation: "now that he is dead, you must consider yourself the boy's guardian."

"The boy is too young to take to sea," Edward said.

"Too young!" my grandfather spluttered, "why you went off to sea at fourteen yourself!"

"*That* was different," Edward stood up and stretched, apparently ending the conversation.

But neither he nor I bargained for my grandfather's persistence.

"Very well, suit yourself," the old man said peevishly. "You have such a high opinion of yourself that you undervalue others. So you'll never know how much this boy knows. I daresay he knows more than most men. Charles taught him everything he knew. They were as thick as thieves, always together. Why the boy even knows how to work that pump Charles was forever dragging over to Cornwall to clear the water out of their mines."

It is hard to describe the gratitude I felt toward my grandfather at that particular moment. It came as such a surprise to me. He was the last person I would have expected to come to my defence. Because he had goaded my father so much about his lack of interest in earning a living, I had naturally taken sides against him and in doing so, had underestimated him. I had been completely unaware that he knew I had worked so closely with my father or that he knew about the pump. I can see now that in his own way, my grandfather was exceedingly proud of my father, even if he did not understand him.

28

The change in Edward's attitude was so obvious and so sudden that I almost laughed out loud.

"The pump you say?" He looked at me in my corner. "Is this true? Do you know how to work the pump!"

"Certainly," I said as offhandedly as I could. Then I came over to the fire and, tilting my head backward because he was a good head taller than I, looked at him directly. "Do you need it?"

He hesitated for the slightest moment and then said, rather begrudgingly I thought, "Yes."

"Well then, it looks as though I may go then," I said, pressing my advantage.

"Yes, it looks like you might be useful after all," my uncle forced a smile. "And now I'll have the papers."

Chapter Six

My uncle moved quickly. We left Shilston the day after he arrived. It took us the rest of the first day and the next morning to pack my father's pump. The pipes had to be taken apart, wrapped in flannel and stowed in crates. The crates were then loaded onto the coach along with my few clothes, books and what were now *my* surveying instruments. Although it was noon, Edward would not stay to eat so Annie packed us a basket of food. To make up for the shortness of his visit, Edward withdrew from one of his pockets a magnificent necklace set with tiny green gems which he gave to Annie and to my grandfather he gave a ring with a large red stone.

Annie was overcome. The rancour she felt toward Edward melted.

"Oh sir, these are beautiful. What are they?"

"Emeralds," Edward said carelessly.

"Emeralds," Annie breathed reverently. "Why I'll feel like Queen Anne herself." She fastened the necklace carefully around her neck, stuck out her chest and strutted comically around the room.

My grandfather reacted differently. He held his ruby ring up to the firelight, studying its bloodred transparency.

"This looks Spanish to me," he muttered.

"Does it matter?" Edward said lightly.

My grandfather grunted. "I suppose not. They're the enemy after all. And whatever you take from the enemy is fair game."

He was referring of course to the continuing war between England and Spain.

Edward had also given me a pouch containing a hundred pounds of gold. The same amount was promised me at the summer's end after I had proved my usefulness. I took the money gleefully, ignorant of the fact that I would have no opportunity to spend it where we were going. So it was that I left Shilston in high spirits. My enthusiasm far outweighed any twinge about leaving my grandfather, Annie or the manor house where I grew up. I was conscious only of making a new start, of earning my own way, of setting forth on the biggest adventure of my life.

The ride over the bumpy, rutted roads to Dartmouth was tedious and uneventful. Conversation was impossible; one had to yell over the squeaking wheels to be heard at all. Moreover it was difficult to sit still since we were so often jolted about on our seats. We arrived in Dartmouth at nightfall and went straight to Edward's ship. It had become so dark that I could just make out its shape but not its name, which I already knew was *The Queen's Privateer*. The ship seemed enormous, its prow towering above us in the dark, its masthead a mountain of canvas and wood. As far as I could see, my uncle's ship seemed to be the only one anchored at the quay. At the

31

time this did not strike me as odd. In his early days as a seaman in the Royal Navy, my uncle had berthed at Portsmouth, but in later years, after he had become a Captain in the Merchant Navy, he usually anchored at Liverpool, a busy commercial port where he traded his cargo. I was far too excited to wonder why he now chose to anchor at Dartmouth which was a small port compared to the others and usually passed by.

As soon as the horses clattered to a stop beside the quay, a giant of a man I recognized as Billy Boles came down the gangplank. He glanced at me critically as I stood clutching my satchel in one hand and Annie's basket of uneaten food in the other.

"And what's this wet-earred whelp doin' 'ere?" he demanded.

"Charles is dead," Edward announced. "Robin understands the pump and has been trained in engineering. He will be his father's substitute."

Billy Boles grunted. "I don't like it. This is no time to coddle a young brat what's never been to sea."

Edward looked at the first mate coolly, "I am not asking you to like it. And as Captain I hardly need your opinion."

"We're in this together like you said," Billy Boles muttered. "It ain't like it was."

"Nothing is ever like it was," my uncle replied testily. "Now get Hinds and Wharton to unload these crates. I want them carefully stowed beneath deck and these cases as well. Then pay off the driver."

While Billy Boles went about these duties with sullen hostility, my uncle took me by the arm and steered me up the gangplank.

"Come along, Robin. I'll find you a bed for the night. You can bunk with Powderlegs. He seldom uses his cabin but sleeps in the dispensary instead."

He led me along the deck. I could see as we walked

swiftly along that there were bodies huddled together on one side of us but it was too dark to see who they were or how many of them there were. Several crewmen stood back as we walked past them down a flight of stairs and along a narrow passage lit only by one lantern. Edward stopped in front of a door at the far end of this corridor, took out a set of keys, unlocked the door and stepped inside a tiny room. I followed, squinting to see in the dark. The lights from the quay could be seen from the porthole providing just enough illumination for me to make out the presence of two bunks, a sea chest and a bucket. My uncle took a candle from its holder on the wall, went into the companionway to light it from the lantern there and returned.

"Now make yourself comfortable. You have Annie's food there in the basket. I suggest you eat and go straight to bed."

"But I thought I'd explore the ship," I protested. It was all so new to me and I wanted to get my bearings as soon as possible.

"That I cannot allow," my uncle said smoothly. "We sail tomorrow. The night before we sail I always permit my crew to celebrate. They become wild and rowdy when they are into the rum and are likely to be quick with a knife or bully a young lad who happens to pass by. It is far better for you to stay here tonight."

I had heard tales of drunken seamen and was not anxious to tangle with any of them, especially Billy Boles who had already shown his dislike of me.

"In any case, you would not be able to see much in the dark, would you?"

I looked at my uncle warily. In the candlelight his handsome face had taken on the appearance of a sharp-featured, cunning fox and I found myself again fearing him. Yet I had to agree he was right.

"No," I conceded.

"Very well then. To make sure you are well protected I shall lock the door." With this Edward turned swiftly and left the room, closing the heavy oak door behind him. I heard the key click in the lock. I tried the handle. Yes, it was locked. I was safe.

I went to the tiny porthole and looked out onto the quay. In the lamplight, I could see the dim outline of two men carrying one of the crates up the gangplank. I heard scraping noises as they dragged it along the deck. I sat down on the bunk, aware of how tired I was, and for the first time that day I was somewhat homesick for the warm hearth of Shilston. I reached into Annie's basket for some of her bread and cheese. When I had eaten, I extinguished the candle and crawled into the top bunk. Even in my sleepy state I remembered I was supposed to be sharing the tiny cabin with Powderlegs and I was certain a man whose legs were cut off above the knees would not be able to use the upper bunk.

But I was alone all night. In spite of the unfamiliar creaking of the wooden ship, I was soon asleep. I slept soundly until sometime during the night when I awakened suddenly. There had been a scream. I was sure of it. An agonized scream as if someone had suddenly been struck dead. I sat upright in bed hitting my head on the beam overhead with a sickening thud. In spite of the sudden pain in my forehead I was aware of a scuffling sound, a few shouts and then silence. I tensed my body, straining to hear more but there was no other sound. I decided that there must have been a fight. One of the crew had probably stabbed another in his drunkenness. How relieved I was that my uncle had locked my door. At least I was out of harm's way. I went back to sleep, completely unaware that what the locked door really meant was that I was a prisoner.

Chapter Seven

As the grey light of early morning filtered through the porthole I awoke again, this time to the sounds of activity above. There was the rush of footsteps, the creak of wood and the clang of metal followed by loud thumps as something hard hit the deck. The ship lurched suddenly and a shiver went down its mammoth wooden spine. I felt myself being rocked slightly. We were moving!

Hastily I slipped out of my bunk and peered through the porthole. The round window was sealed shut and would not open. Still I could see the water widening between us and the quay. The thumps must have been the anchors being heaved onto the deck. I went to the door and tried to open it before I remembered that it was locked. I banged loudly and yelled to be let out but there was too much commotion for me to be heard. How cheated I felt! My first time aboard a sailing ship and I was cooped up in a tiny cabin. I kept banging on the door with my fists but to no avail. Finally, I resigned myself to keeping my nose pressed against the porthole. I could just see some of the boats that were helping us to move away from the quay and out of the harbour.

Eventually, I heard footsteps down the hall. I kicked the door hard to make sure I was heard, and was soon rewarded. A key scraped in the lock, the knob turned, the door opened and there in the corridor stood my uncle himself. He seemed amused by my agitation and in a hurry.

"Did you sleep well?" he asked but did not wait for an answer. "We've cleared the harbour. As soon as we've finished raising the sails, we'll be underway."

I was about to splutter my indignation about being locked in for so long but Edward had already passed on to his cabin. I dashed up the stairs two at a time to the quarterdeck where I was met by an exhilarating surge of sea air. I will never forget that first moment I stood on the deck. I watched fascinated as the last of the sails were raised. The masts swayed above me and the white sails billowed full and round in the breeze. I felt myself dwarfed by their height. Because I had never before been on a sailing ship, *The Queen's Privateer* seemed enormous to me when in fact it was a third-rater; a medium-size ship, carrying only seventy-four guns on two decks.

I left the quarterdeck and went up another flight of stairs to the poop deck at the back of the ship. There I stood looking down on the ship's wake, that white foam pathway that followed us throughout our voyage. For a long time I stared into the wake, marvelling at how easily the sea opened up, allowing us easy passage through her, and just as easily folded in upon herself behind us, leaving no trace of having been passed over at all.

Eventually I made my way downstairs past the bulwarks mounted at intervals with cannons securely lashed to the ship's sides, back down to the maindeck. What I saw there stopped me cold. Among the many nautical sounds unfamiliar to my ear was another sound, that of the irregular clinking of metal. I did not know its origin until I saw them on the maindeck: eighty-five black slaves chained together. I had never seen slaves before and I was horrified by the sight of them. They were naked except for ragged blankets and a tattered assortment of cast-off jackets and trousers. None wore shoes or socks though the spring breezes that billowed our sails were raw with cold. I knew that they must have come from Africa, one of the hottest areas in the world. Would that not mean that they would suffer more from the cold? They took no notice of me but remained huddled together on the deck for whatever warmth they could gain from one another. In any case, I noticed there was very little room for them to stretch out had they wanted to. Some still slept, others sat, hunched over, eyes closed, their bodies swaying with the movement of the ship. They seemed unconscious of where they were or that they were aboard a vessel bound for America. Each man was heavily manacled with a chain secured to his ankle with a thick iron band. I could see that in many cases their ankles were chafed and red from the scrape of the band.

I stood watching the slaves for a long time, immobilized by my own revulsion. Suddenly I realized I felt sick to my stomach. All I wanted to do was lie down. I had started back to my cabin for this purpose when my eye caught sight of a red stain on the deck. It was fresh and still sticky. I knew at once that it was blood.

Chapter Eight

The bloodstain on the maindeck made my stomach feel
worse. I hurried downstairs to my cabin as fast as I
could. Maybe if I lay down, I'd feel better. But I was not
going to have a chance to find out.

As soon as I reached the door, I saw that the bottom
bunk was occupied. Powderlegs was sprawled, as well as
a legless man can sprawl, on top of the blanket, his arms
crossed behind his head. With his wrinkled brow and
quick watchful eyes he reminded me more than ever of a
monkey.

"Well, now," he greeted me, "we meet again. I hear,
boy, that we's to be roommates."

"Yes," I said, and sat down on the sea chest. My knees
were about to give out completely.

"Glad to have you aboard," he said amiably, leaning
over and clapping me on the back in a friendly way.

He seemed genuinely glad to see me, so different from
Billy Boles' hostile reaction to my presence aboard ship.

I decided it might help take my mind off my stomach to talk to him.

"Uncle says you usually sleep in the dispensary," I said.

"Ah yes, that I do. It saves me using my wood on the steps. It ain't easy gettin' up and down with these 'ere crutches. But I couldn't listen to that man groan no more. No siree. Just had to get away from him, I did." Whereupon he pulled a half-empty flask of rum from his waistcoat pocket and drank deeply, smacking his lips with satisfaction.

"What man?" I asked.

He seemed surprised that I didn't know. "Why the man that cut off his foot, of course."

"A man cut off his foot?" I repeated the words because I had difficulty believing them. "That must have been the scream I heard."

"That it were. Poor wretch. Right off his head he was. I tied up the tubes so's he wouldn't bleed so much. Must a got holt of one of the axes tied to the bulwarks. Got the chain right off his foot. Nearly overboard he was, afore they got him."

"You mean he was a slave?"

"Yes siree!"

"I thought it was a fight between two crewmen. I mean I know they were drinking and fighting."

"Weren't no fightin' in the crew," Powderlegs said, "no drinkin' neither. The Cap'n don't allow no drinkin' the night afore we sails. We gets our rum when we gets where we's goin' but not the night afore we sails. He never does that. One of his rules it is."

I said nothing. If what Powderlegs said was true, my uncle had lied to me about locking the door. He had led me to believe that his crew would be drunk and wild last night, so he could keep me confined to my cabin until we sailed. Yet if it were true that rum was rationed, why was Powderlegs drinking it?

"You have rum," I pointed out.

"Yes siree, that I have. *I* gets all the rum I want. It ain't rationed to *me*. A surgeon needs rum for settin' bones and the like. It's medicine you might say. Poured a whole bottle into the slave I did. He took it meek as a lamb he did, his leg was hurtin' him so bad." Powderlegs slapped his leg stumps, "I know how it feels, I do. Yes siree. It sure hurts." He shook his head, remembering his own pain.

"Do they ever get away?"

Powderlegs looked blank. "Who?"

"The slaves."

"Never. Unless you count jumpin' overboard in the middle of the ocean and not bein' able to swim a stroke."

"They do that?"

"Not on *The Queen's Privateer* they don't 'cause the Cap'n keeps 'em chained for their own good. But I seed men do it afore. Long time ago. Yes siree. Watched many a black man kill hisself that way. Once I was on a ship and six of 'em tried to take over. Cap'n ordered 'em overboard. Into shark water it was too. They got ate up fast, they did. I'll tell you that."

I shuddered. "It's not right!"

"Well, all's I can say is that if the Cap'n wants slaves it's all right by me. The Cap'n knows best, I can tell you. The Cap'n and me, we been together over ten years. Why, he even up and married me little sister."

This surprised me. I hadn't known my uncle was married, but then it was becoming increasingly clear how little I knew him. Sometimes relatives are more strange to us than strangers.

"Most Cap'ns woulda dumped me after me legs got blowed off at Vigo Bay," Powderlegs was saying, "but the Cap'n says, 'Roger, we been in this together and we'll stay together'."

Although I still felt sick to my stomach, I was alert enough to recognize Vigo Bay. Nearly everyone knew the story of the battle in Vigo Bay. Two years ago English and Dutch ships had cornered the Spanish and French ships there just off the coast of Spain. There had been a fierce battle. A vast treasure had been involved. It was said to be the largest ever to have come across the Atlantic in Spanish galleons. Even though the English and Dutch had defeated the Spanish, it was reported that most of the gold had sunk to the bottom of the bay.

So Powderlegs and my uncle had been there. Maybe with his tongue loosened by drink, Powderlegs would tell me more.

"So it was at Vigo Bay that you lost your legs," I said casually, careful not to appear too eager to hear more.

"That it were. Nearly went down with the ship, I did 'til the Cap'n pulled me off."

It was obvious Powderlegs thought my uncle some sort of hero.

"Then my uncle's ship went down in Vigo Bay, did it?"

"No, we was on the enemy ship. The three of us: the Cap'n, Billy and me. It was goin' down fast. But we had to get the gold, see. There it was. Them Spanish dogs, a cowardly lot they was, jumped ship, leavin' them chests jest sittin' there." Powderlegs' voice took on a feverish quality, "I never seed anythin' like it. No one could see nuthin'. Fires everywhere. Smoke all over. Couldn't see yer hand in front of yer face. This gall'yun, a beauty she was, 'cept she was on fire, she jest glides by, empty, all her crew gone, like some bloody ghost ship. Them Spanish dogs had dragged them chests from outta somewheres. Were goin' to throw 'em overboard so's we wouldn't get 'em. But the ship musta caught fire and

41

they jumped into the water like a bunch a scared rabbits.

"All 'cept one. He jest sat there on a chest and glowered at us like a bulldog. So we boards her, see. We ain't afraid. There's them chests waitin' fer somebody to lift 'em off. All's between us and them is the bulldog. Don't matter to the Cap'n. He puts his pistol 'tween that dog's eyes and fires. 'Course he dies right on the spot. I woulda tossed him in the sea myself but the Cap'n ain't one to let anyone get in his way.

"So we carries off them chests. Jest like that. Jest like it were a present. All my years at sea I never seed anythin' like it. We sailed outta there, through the boom and none of the others knew that gold wasn't on the bottom of the bay somewheres. Even the rest of our crew didn't know. Only the three of us." Powderlegs began to laugh, a shrill chattering sound like a monkey high in the branches of a tree flaunting his private joke over the other jungle creatures.

I was astounded by this revelation and very excited. I knew I must keep him talking. I had to learn everything I could from him while he was still drinking.

"Your legs, tell me about your legs."

"See, we was comin' off with the last chest. I was still on the gall'yun I was. The Cap'n had jest crossed onto our ship when Wham! The deck blows up! Them Spaniards didn't take their gold but they was makin' sure no one else got holt of it. 'Cept we fooled 'em. We got it all off but for that one chest. It went into the water. I nearly went into the drink too 'cept for the Cap'n. He grabs holt of my arms and pulls me over. I never forget that. No siree. Saved my life he did. Fixed me up afterwards. 'Roger,' he says to me, 'you lost your legs but you still got two good hands you can use. You can be ship's surgeon from now on'." Powderlegs held up his hands,

now shaking from too much drink. "See, I still got two good hands." He stuck them in front of my face. "Nuthin' wrong with 'em is there? Yes siree, I still can tie up a wound as good as anyone!"

I looked at Powderlegs' hands. They were creased and ringed with black, the fingernails long, ragged and dirty. The thought of his using those filthy hands to tie up a wound proved too much for my stomach and I suddenly found myself bent over a bucket, retching miserably into it.

Chapter Nine

After I was thoroughly sick to my stomach, Powderlegs offered me a swig of rum from his flask.

"The best cure there is," he cackled.

I shook my head; rum was the last thing my stomach needed. While Powderlegs put the flask to his own mouth, I crawled onto the top bunk. I knew I must concentrate on the information he had given me but for the time being I wanted to escape the miseries of being seasick even more. So I slept.

When I awoke, Powderlegs had gone. He must have told my uncle about my condition because presently Edward appeared in the doorway.

"Now, Robin," he said briskly, "lying in bed is no way to get your sea legs. The best thing to do is to get up and move about above deck. Go to the galley and ask the cook for bread and water. Then eat it slowly."

"But where is the galley?" I asked plaintively. I was used to having Annie fetch me water when I was sick and could not resist feeling sorry for myself now that I was ill without her.

"Ask any of the crew. They'll tell you," Edward retorted and passed on down the passageway.

I thought my uncle extremely cold for not showing me more sympathy, but I got up off my bunk and though I found my knees so weak I was sure I would collapse before I got to the stairs, I managed to get up on deck and eventually located the galley. One of the cooks allowed me a hunk of bread and a jug of fresh water. At first he would not give me anything but when I told him my uncle had sent me, he consented. He was as unpleasant and unfriendly as the other crew members I had seen. Like the others he wore no uniform. With the exception of my uncle and the first mate, none of them did. Although the crew was closely disciplined and thoroughly experienced, the men wore a rag-tag assortment of jackets, shirts and trousers. Some were clean-shaven, others had grizzled beards, some wore caps, even turbans, most were bareheaded. Altogether they looked like the scrapings of half a dozen ports. I decided they were a group to be avoided and that is exactly what I tried to do.

After several hours above deck in the fresh salt air I felt much better. I became used to the ship's steady rocking. My mind gradually separated itself from my stomach and I was able to think with more concentration about the information Powderlegs had given me.

If what he had told me was true, and I had no reason to believe otherwise, my uncle, along with Powderlegs and Billy Boles, was in possession of a vast treasure, one that most people, including the British Admiralty, thought was in Spain at the bottom of Vigo Bay. That being the case, the treasure was somewhere aboard this ship, probably in my uncle's cabin.

This would explain my uncle's haste in leaving Shilston: one would not leave a ship laden with treasure unless it was absolutely necessary and then only for the shortest possible time. It explained his choice of a smaller port like Dartmouth where his ship was less likely to be noticed, and it also explained why he had come with Powderlegs and Billy Boles to see my father a year ago in early spring. By that time Edward would have decided where to hide his treasure. And he wanted it hidden according to a carefully worked out, foolproof plan so that no one but himself could get at it. And what better man for such a task than his own brother who was a brilliant engineer? It also explained why my father agreed to keep the project secret. He knew about the treasure. He also knew that his brother was a pirate. Not an ordinary pirate but a pirate nonetheless.

By 1704 pirates had earned a grim reputation. They were considered no better than common thieves. Most people, including myself, thought of them as bullying rogues who carried knives between their teeth and pistols in their belts. My uncle, however, did not look like a pirate. His chin and hair were neatly kept, his clothes clean and stylish. Nor was he wild and coarse in his manner. He kept aloof from his crew, dispatching orders through his first mate and in this way ran a tightly controlled ship. Rum was rationed and weapons were kept under lock and key except for Billy Boles who always carried two pistols in his belt. He paid his crew better than most and it was for this reason that they tolerated his strict measures.

My uncle had been a privateer for many years. That meant he had his Letters of Marque from The Crown which provided him with written permission to board enemy ships in the name of Queen Anne. He was then able to strip the ships of their wealth, scuttle or burn them, even kill everybody aboard—as long as he gave Her Majesty a share of the plunder, which often meant

47

more than half of it. If he did not share the booty with the Queen, he was no longer a privateer but a pirate. My uncle apparently saw no good reason for turning pirate until Vigo Bay. When those rich chests floated past on the empty galleon, he could not resist the temptation to take the booty and flee, protected by the smoke and confusion of battle. After that there was no turning back. There was no place, no port he could enter without fear of his secret being discovered until the treasure was made secure. To date he had one big advantage and that was that the British, Dutch, Spanish and French all thought the treasure was at the bottom of Vigo Bay and therefore had no reason to hunt down *The Queen's Privateer*.

When I realized the awful truth of my uncle's piracy, all I could think about was the danger involved. What if we were caught? We had a long passage ahead of us, weeks at sea. What if one of the enemy ships or even the British Admiralty somehow found out about the treasure and pursued us? They would open fire and either board us, or damage us so badly we would sink to the bottom of the sea. I remembered with horror that only three years before, Captain William Kidd, the famous privateer-turned-pirate, had been caught and hanged for his crimes, his blackened and mutilated body left dangling in chains at Execution Dock as a warning to other pirates. I knew if we were seized, I might escape hanging because of my age, but I would most certainly end up in Newgate Prison and everybody in England knew that many who went behind those walls disappeared forever.

As I stood on deck steadying myself against the railing and surveying the vast empty expanse of sea stretching toward an unknown horizon, I shook with fear. I did not think my situation could possibly get worse. I had yet to learn that the greatest danger was not enemy ships or Newgate gaolers but my uncle himself.

Chapter Ten

After I had pieced together the facts as best I could from
what Powderlegs had told me, I began to wonder, once
again, about the role my father had played in the whole
affair. Would he have gone with Edward if he had known
he was a pirate? Was he aware of the danger involved?
Or was he kept prisoner as I was until it was too late to
turn back? I knew the treasure itself would not have interested him, unless he was more affected than I knew
by my grandfather's constant reminders that he was a
poor man. Perhaps he had decided it was a chance to become wealthy at last and he could return to Shilston with
a sackful of gold which he could with great ceremony lay
at his father's feet, saying as he did so, "Here is your
money! Now let me hear no more about my lack of it!"

I did not think that was likely except in my own imagination. The truth was that my father probably over-
looked his brother's piracy because he was presented
with an engineering challenge he could not resist. I knew

the challenge must have been great. Beyond that, I knew nothing. The time had come to find out. If I was to continue what my father had started I needed time to study all his plans. The sooner the treasure was in the ground, the safer we would all be—or so I thought.

Full of resolution I marched boldly up to my uncle's cabin, my heart pounding. To my surprise the door was slightly ajar. Was he expecting me?

My uncle was very clever at assessing people. I will not say he "understood" them because understanding, to me, means compassion and concern for others and he had neither of these qualities. I mean he was shrewd in measuring a person's value to him. I suppose it was this ability that helped make him successful. In any case he seemed to be waiting for me that day as if he knew all along I would be knocking on his door. As soon as I had done so, he called for me to enter.

So great was my amazement at the interior of Edward's cabin that I momentarily forgot what I had come for. His quarters resembled more a room in a palace than a cabin aboard ship. The walls were panelled in carved rosewood, the floor carpeted with a thick Persian rug covered with bird and flower designs. On the walls were elaborate candelabras. The portholes were curtained in velvet, as was the large bed in the corner.

My uncle was sitting at a wooden desk that was as elaborately carved and polished as the other furniture in the room. On it was a silver ink pot and quill as well as maps and drawings which I recognized as my father's.

"I see you have found your sea legs," he said.

I nodded.

"Then you must treat yourself to some figs. They're very good." My uncle gestured to a low table beside the desk which held a silver bowl heaped with dried figs, a silver flagon of wine and silver goblets.

50

I took a handful of figs and sat down, warily. I mistrusted my uncle's courtesy.

"I think I should learn more about the project if I am to use my father's pump," I said slowly. "I don't even know where we're going."

"You are quite right," he agreed. "You do not know where we are going or why, so I shall show you. Come here."

I went behind the desk and stood behind him. He unrolled a small map and held it open for me to see. I looked at the map. It was simply drawn with few details. There was an island, a long "S"-shaped island with deep coves at one end.

"This island is our destination," my uncle announced.

"But where is it?" I asked, "I see no names on the map."

"It is precisely because it has no name that we are going there. It is one of many nameless islands in a large bay off the coast of Acadie in North America. It is a remote part of the world far from the major shipping lanes."

"Are there no people there?"

"A few traders come and go along the coast but that is all."

"What about Indians?"

My uncle shrugged. "They are there on the mainland," his finger brushed the left hand corner of the map, "but they are savages. For our intents and purposes we may consider the area uninhabited."

"Then why are we going there?"

"To build this." My uncle pulled a large chart from beneath the map. The drawing was my father's work. It showed a deep shaft near the bottom of which was a vault. I knew what the vault was but I thought it wise not to let Edward see that I did. Besides I wanted to know exactly how much he would tell me so I said simply, "What is it?"

My uncle took a few figs from the bowl, fastidiously removing their stems; his eyes never left my face. Finally he said, "And what do you think it is?"

My earlier bluff had worked. He was wondering how much I knew. I could see it was to be a game of cat and mouse. I shrugged, "It's a mine. You have discovered a gold mine on this small out-of-the-way island."

When he heard this, my uncle threw back his head and laughed. It was a high hooting laugh, an unpleasant sound, mocking my ignorance. Finally his mirth subsided and he said with painstaking slowness as if he were talking to a small child, "Robin, I am a wealthy man. Very wealthy. Privateering has paid me well, especially during the past few years. Naturally I wish to make my wealth secure. This shaft," he tapped the chart with his forefinger, "is a treasure vault, a storage vault you might say, which we will build on the island. It is there that I intend to put my wealth."

I had not expected him to tell me more than that. Obviously my uncle did not consider himself a pirate, and I've wondered since how many pirates did. I am sure he thought that after so many years of service to the Crown, he deserved the Spanish gold chance brought his way.

"Now your part in this project, aside from checking your father's calculations, is to assemble the pump, and teach me how to work it. To do this you will have to become thoroughly familiar with all the details of your father's design, especially the tunnelling and the floodgate."

Tunnelling, floodgate. This was the first I had heard of these. My uncle extended the papers containing my father's designs and I took them eagerly, anxious to learn more. I wanted to understand fully the details of this project which had captured my father's imagination. And I was curious about Edward. Perhaps by studying the designs I might uncover some clue about his overall plans.

Chapter Eleven

It was on a warm morning in early summer that we finally reached our destination, sailing into the large bay Edward had shown me with its nameless islands. As my father's sketches had suggested, there were hundreds of islands. All morning we sailed the watery labyrinth between them. The islands were as irregularly shaped and sized as pieces of a jigsaw puzzle; some were more than a mile or two across, others were mere rock outcroppings. I scanned their shorelines closely for some sign of life, hopeful I might at least sight a rabbit or a squirrel but there was nothing. These islands it seemed were as new and untrammelled as they had been at Creation.

Most of the islands we passed, except the very smallest ones, were heavily treed, mostly with fir. There was one exception, that being an "S"-shaped island close to the mainland: it was covered with a thick stand of oak trees. And it was in a small deep cove at the tip of this island that we dropped anchor.

I wanted to go ashore immediately. After the long weeks at sea I could hardly wait to set foot on dry land again and to explore the island. But Edward would not permit it. Our disembarkment, he said, was to be orderly and methodical. Because of the depth of the water we were able to anchor fairly close in. I knew I could easily swim the distance to shore. Nevertheless I did as my uncle bade me and waited with the others while Billy Boles and twenty crewmen lowered two Jolly-boats into the water and rowed ashore. Once there, they disappeared into the bushes that skirted the water's edge. Soon they reappeared, dragging a large wooden raft or platform to the shore. This done they disappeared again, reappearing as before with another raft. They did this four times more until they had six platforms lined up along the beach. One by one the platforms were pushed into the water and lashed to each other in such fashion that they made a floating wharf stretching from the shore to *The Queen's Privateer*. This I recognized as one of my father's ideas to provide easy movement of men and equipment between ship and shore. Obviously the platforms had been made the summer before and concealed in the bushes.

Before we were allowed ashore, my uncle announced that there was to be a double ration of rum that evening to mark the end of a successful crossing and the beginning of the summer's work. For this reason I decided in the back of my mind that I might sleep on the island if the night proved warm enough. Certainly the day was balmy. Even though it was mid-afternoon, the air was warm, almost hot. This surprised me, having taken North America quite literally by its name.

I went ashore soon after, taking with me some bread and cheese and a blanket, and made my way through the underbrush uphill. Because I had studied my father's

55

Oak
Island

drawings in great detail, I knew exactly where I was going and what I might expect to find. At the top of the hill was a small clearing with a large oak tree in the middle. On the ground beneath was a platform about fourteen feet square covered with canvas concealing the shaft which had been dug more than one hundred feet into the ground, with platforms constructed every ten feet to the bottom. Near the bottom of the shaft was my uncle's treasure vault.

There was nothing crude about my father's plan. His was no pick and shovel method of burying treasure. He had chosen this island because it had the ideal geography for his design: a hill rising several feet above sea level between two good coves, and a natural sink hole which made the construction of the shaft easier. With the shaft and treasure vault completed last summer, my father's plan now called for a tunnel to be built from the shaft just below the vault to the sea.

The tunnel was to be two-and-a-half feet wide and four feet high and would rise at an angle of twenty-two and a half degrees to the sea. It was to be built by two crews, one digging from the shaft outwards towards the sea, the other from the sea inwards towards the shaft.

The crews working outward from the shaft would dig the tunnel to within a short distance of the beach where they would then put in place a floodgate constructed of heavy timber, caulked to make it watertight. The floodgate would serve as a watergate or bulkhead to keep the sea from entering the tunnel and shaft before construction was completed and the treasure put in place. The floodgate would be lowered through a small access shaft built down from the surface. Once it was in place the crews would put stones into the tunnel to help keep the walls from collapsing when the sea water was allowed in.

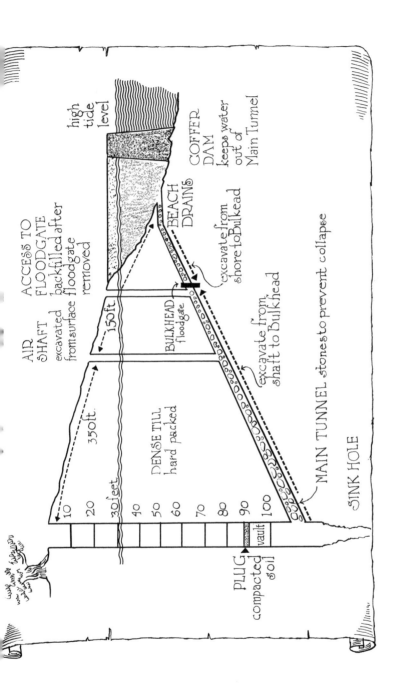

AIR SHAFT excavated from surface

ACCESS TO FLOODGATE backfilled after floodgate removed

high tide level

COFFER DAM keeps water out of Main Tunnel

150 ft.

350 ft.

BEACH DRAINS

BULKHEAD floodgate

excavate from shore to Bulkhead

DENSE TILL hard packed

excavate from shaft to Bulkhead

10
20
30 feet
40
50
60
70
80
90
100

MAIN TUNNEL stones to prevent collapse

SINK HOLE

PLUG compacted soil

vault

The crews digging in from the sea to the floodgate would first build a cofferdam to help keep back the sea. When the tunnel was connected to the sea, the cofferdam would be removed, allowing the water to flow into the tunnel until it reached the floodgate.

After the treasure was placed in the vault, the shaft would be filled in with loose soil. The plan called for a layer of hard soil to be packed above the treasure vault. This would act as a plug to keep the water from rising any higher. Once the rest of the shaft was filled in, the floodgate in the tunnel would be taken out, permitting the sea water to move into the tunnel and up against the plug in the shaft.

The purpose of my father's plan was to use the sea to protect Edward's store of riches. Were intruders for any reason to suspect there was treasure buried on the island and dig into the shaft, they would never be able to enter the vault because when they dug deep enough to be near the vault area, they would strike the plug of hard soil. Once this plug was dug into there would be nothing to keep the sea water in the tunnel and the bottom part of the shaft from rising sixty feet to sea level, thus flooding out the diggers.

There was a way to get the treasure out, of course, but only someone who could put my father's engineering ingenuity into effect would know how. It was intended that when Edward was ready to retrieve his gold, that he drop the floodgate into position in the tunnel before entering the main shaft. After the sea had been shut off it would be possible to dig out the shaft, advancing from platform to platform to the treasure. The sea water that remained in the shaft and the tunnel would, of course, be taken out by my father's pump.

Although the plan worked on sound principles of logic and simplicity, it was not going to be easy to build. The

60

construction of the tunnel was bound to be risky and dangerous. But I did not want to think about risks and dangers on this warm spring afternoon. It was my first day in America and I was eager to explore my surroundings.

I left the clearing and cut through the woods towards the shore, noticing as I did numerous stumps where oak trees had been felled. I struck out along the shore, satisfying the urge to get as far away as possible from the ship. After so long aboard *The Queen's Privateer* with a crew I neither knew nor trusted, all I wanted was to be free of them. If, as Edward claimed, the island was uninhabited, then I was perfectly safe. I found walking along the shore required concentration. The way was rocky: in places it disappeared altogether in which case I crawled through the thick brush alongside until the shore resumed itself. I went on until I reached the island's wide, blunt end. As I rounded this bend to the island's other side, I was surprised to discover how close the island came to the mainland. In fact there was but a narrow channel, a stone's throw, between them.

I could see a beach of white sand on the opposite shore, something the island seemed to lack. So far it had been rocky all the way round with only small patches of sand here and there. How inviting the beach looked, the smooth fine sand stretching nearly all the way to the woods. The sea between was green and sparkling in the sunlight.

Hastily I stripped off my clothes and waded into the sea. The water was not unbearably cold; cradled as it was in the channel, the sun had warmed it to a considerable degree. I dived in and swam to the opposite shore where I flopped onto the grey-white sand. How good the sand felt. I dug into its warmth. Carefully, starting at my feet, I mounded the sand over my ankles, legs and torso until except for my head, I was completely covered. Then I leaned my head back and closed my eyes against the sun, feeling more content than I had in a very long time. At last I was well and truly in North America. And how peaceful it was. There was no sound except waves lapping the beach. There was nothing around me but water, sand, trees and sun. Relaxed by the thought that I had this shining world to myself, I went to sleep— only to be awakened moments later by a cold nose touching my forehead.

Chapter Twelve

The day before *The Queen's Privateer* arrived at its island destination, a young Indian boy by the name of Actaudin was splashing in the water far down the coast. He was trying, unsuccessfully, to swim. Though his people camped each summer along the coast where fishing was plentiful, few of them knew how to move on top of the water without a canoe. His mother and father had both drowned in the waters of the mighty ocean when their canoe overturned.

It had happened eight summers ago when Actaudin was six. His eleven-year-old brother, Tagalak, had been the first one in the Micmac village to see the empty canoe being washed ashore from the sandbar where their parents had gone to spear lobsters. Their bodies had never been found. The sagamore or chief of their tribe, Alsoosit, whose own sons were grown men, took Tagalak and Actaudin into his wigwam to live with his old wife Atkegwee and himself.

During the days of the death-feast which followed the drowning, Alsoosit spoke long and with grief about the hunger of the sea. It had swallowed so many of the Micmac people. Every summer when they journeyed to their camp beside the sea, someone in their tribe either drowned or came close to drowning. It was a common sight to see the drowned victim tied upsidedown in a tree. Tobacco smoke was forced into his lungs and if he disgorged all the water he had swallowed, he lived. If not, he died.

Alsoosit said the Micmac's Creator, Kesulk, had made the sea so that in exchange for an abundant harvest of clams, oysters, scallops and lobsters, he expected a sacrifice from his people. Actaudin did not think this had to be so. He vowed that the sea would never take him the way it had taken his parents. He would learn to swim. He knew it could be done because he had seen white men do it.

He remembered the summer before when some white men first came to the cove. They came from a floating island that remained far out, beyond the small waves. The men brought with them coloured beads, a hatchet, and a bright red cap for Alsoosit. For these they wanted the skins of the beaver, bear and moose, which his people had in great number.

The Great Chief, Glooscap, who lived in The Land Beyond the Skies, had told of the white man's coming. Glooscap was a giant who long ago had come out of the sky in a stone canoe. He performed many good deeds for his people. One day he gathered his friends, the Micmac and the animals, about him. He told them he was returning to The Land Beyond the Skies because the white men were coming.

Alsoosit allowed the white men to stay in their camp for most of the summer so that they could trade together. On the evening before the white men were to leave, Alsoosit invited two of them to sit with him in front of his wigwam and share his pipe. One of the men, who was not clean-shaven like the Micmac but had much hair growing from his chin, brought brown water in a skin bag for them to drink. When it came Alsoosit's turn to drink, he spat upon the ground. It was bad water, he said. It was not clear and sweet like that which is people drank from streams but fire water which burned his throat.

When Alsoosit spat upon the ground, the bearded man took the skin bag and drank all of the remaining brown water. This angered the other white man. He began to hit the bearded man with his fists until he ran into the sea. He went straight out where his feet could not touch the sand. Actaudin watched, expecting him to drown as his parents had but the man began to move on top of the sea, his legs hitting the water like the beaver's tail. On and on he went until he reached the floating island. Actaudin knew the white men did not call it floating island. That was the Micmac way of explaining what they had never seen before. The white man used the word, "ship." It was one of many words the bearded man had taught him to speak that summer.

Alsoosit thought the spectacle of the bearded man's swimming was magic, for Glooscap had spoken of the white man's extraordinary power. Actaudin knew it was not so. And he intended to prove it, if only to himself and his dog, Meko. Meko was beside him now, watching his young master with anxious tolerance. He was used to seeing Actaudin flail about in the sea until, exhausted and shivering, he flopped down on the sand, burrowing in its warmth. Meko was nervous around water and liked nothing about these daily swimming excursions. Only when Actaudin had returned to the safety of the beach did he allow himself to relax his vigilance and stretch out on the sand.

Actaudin closed his eyes and listened to the rhythmic fall of waves on the beach. There was a slight shuffling across the sand and then Meko's low growl.

"Well, well, what have we here? A fish washed in by the tide or a giant sand crab?" said a voice beside him.

Actaudin opened his eyes to see his older brother standing tall and brown beside him and then he quickly closed them again.

Tagalak gave the sandy body a gentle shove with his bare foot.

"Hmmm. It doesn't speak. It doesn't move when I touch it. Yet it opens its eyes. I think it is a fish and that being so, I should do the kind thing and return it to the sea."

Tagalak bent over to take hold of his brother.

Actaudin leapt up. Sand sprayed in all directions.

"No. No. It's me."

"It's my little brother!" Tagalak said, pretending surprise.

Actaudin glowered at his brother. Ever since he could remember, Tagalak had been a tease and now that he was a few days from getting married, his teasing was worse than ever.

"You knew it all the time."

"Maybe so but I had to be sure. I wouldn't want to send a fish or a sand crab on a special journey, would I?"

Actaudin's eyes widened. A special journey. Was Tagalak going to ask him to hunt for the wedding feast? In their tribe it was the custom for the bridegroom to provide the wedding feast.

"I shall go after a big moose," Tagalak went on "for we have had our fill of clams and oysters and I would like fresh meat for the feast. I want you, little brother, to catch me some eels. We have not had eels this season and they will make a fine treat."

So he was being asked to help and very likely he was the only one who was.

"You can take the small canoe," Tagalak said.

His brother had made two canoes: a larger one he gave to his bride-to-be's father, and a smaller one he used himself. It was part of his preparation for taking a wife.

"Don't you need it?" asked Actaudin.

Tagalak laughed. "Are you suggesting that I paddle through the trees?"

This time Actaudin did not mind being teased. Wasn't Tagalak trusting him with his newly made canoe?

"I know a place of day's journey from here where a narrow stream runs into the sea," Actaudin pointed along the coast. "That is where I shall find the best eels."

"We'll leave early tomorrow. I'll need your help getting things ready," Tagalak said, and assuming Actaudin would follow, he turned to go.

"I'll come," Actaudin called after him, "as soon as I have had one more swim." There was always the chance that this time he really would succeed.

Tagalak retraced his steps. Gone was his usual jocularity. Instead he was stern and serious.

"You had better stop playing about in the water or you will offend Kesulk. If you behave like a fish, you will catch nothing tomorrow."

This time it was Actaudin's turn to tease. Pitching his voice high, he began to mimic the quavering speech of Alsoosit.

"If the soup slips into the fire, you'll have bad luck. If a young woman enters a wigwam where there is bear meat, hunting will be bad. If the bones of the beaver are burned, there will be. . ."

67

"That's enough," Tagalak said sharply, "you must show more respect for the customs of our people."

"Not if they make no sense to me," Actaudin said.

"Ever since time has begun they have worked for us and it is not for a young cub like you to dispute them. Be careful not to fall into your own trap," Tagalak retorted and strode angrily back to camp.

Actaudin said nothing. It was no use. They had had the same argument many times before and always with the same result. Although Tagalak liked to make jokes like a young man, his ideas were those of an old one. He questioned nothing. He did not see that some of the old taboos made no sense. What could learning to swim have to do with poor fishing? Tomorrow he, Actaudin, would catch so many eels he would prove his swimming had not harmed the fishing. He would prove that Tagalak was wrong and he was right.

Chapter Thirteen

During the night a thick fog crept southward along the coast so that when Actaudin emerged from Alsoosit's wigwam at dawn, the cove was shrouded in white mist. Being careful not to waken the old chief and his wife, he picked up his mooseskin robe and beaver pelt which kept him warm while he slept. Tagalak was already up, spreading bear grease generously over his body. He handed the skin pouch to Actaudin. For now, yesterday's angry words were forgotten.

"Here, little brother, help yourself."

Actaudin began greasing his arms and legs: the grease would help keep him warm and prevent flies from biting.

"You will not need as much as I," Tagalak said, "where I am going, the flies come in clouds."

Actaudin knew that the inland lake country where Tagalak was going was infested with flies. The same swamps which fed the moose bred flies. The task ahead of Tagalak would be difficult. Usually the hunting was done by several men. This time Tagalak must do it alone as further proof of his manhood. Actaudin did not envy the ritual his brother must follow in order to marry Wosowek.

Tagalak read his thoughts. "Some day your turn will come, little brother. Have no fear of that."

"Never," Actaudin said. Although he supposed that some day he might take a wife, he did not want to think about it sooner than was absolutely necessary.

"Our mother and father would want you to," Tagalak said gravely, "our people must grow great and strong."

Actaudin did not offer to go with Tagalak. It would be an insult to suggest that he was unable to handle the hunt alone.

"Don't forget, little brother, that my totem is Team, the moose," Tagalak fingered the carved bone amulet around his neck, "I earned the right to wear my father's totem. With it I cannot fail."

The brothers finished greasing their bodies in silence. Tagalak pulled on his leggings, tied them to his belt and pushed his feet into moccasins. Both leggings and moccasins were necessary in the forest; Actaudin needed only a breechclout, moccasins and for now a mooseskin robe over his shoulders against the early morning chill. Because they had eaten well the night before, they were content with drinking leftover soup. As was their custom, the brothers parted without ceremony; each simply went his own way.

With Meko at his heels, Actaudin carried the canoe to the cove and set it carefully on the sand. Then he returned for the beaver pelt and the baskets holding the small bone gorges attached to thin leather thongs which were his fishing lines. The day before he had dug a supply of worms and these he put into the canoe. Arranging

70

the beaver pelt on the bottom as a cushion for Meko and himself, he pushed away from shore and knelt down on the soft fur. He heard the dogs barking on the other side of the camp as they set off with Tagalak.

Actaudin was pleased that the fog had brought a calm sea. In choppy waves the canoe was easily upset but this morning it slid quietly forward, making shiny folds of the water. He kept close to shore until he became aware of a low finger of land pointing toward the sea. It was the burial ground of his forefathers. To give the sacred land a wide berth he made a large arc around it. It was said that the wailings of the dead could draw you underground into The Land of Souls, never to return. Once when he had been snaring rabbits he had gone too close, strangely attracted to the brushwood piled over the graves. He had heard no wailings; no one had called to him. Yet he remembered feeling as if unseen eyes were watching him.

The burial ground was forbidden territory and no one knew he had gone so close. Had he known, Tagalak would have been angry with him, but then Tagalak often was. He seemed to think of himself as his father rather than his brother. Actaudin and Tagalak had not always disagreed about the customs of their people. During the early years Actaudin had accepted his brother's words and those of Alsoosit without question. He was eager to do whatever was expected of him, whether it was around the camp or during the hunt.

But in his twelfth year he began to change. It was then he realized that before he could become a man he must find a totem. Every grown Micmac male had a totem, an animal spirit that guided and protected him. Tagalak had always known that his totem would be Team, the moose, because as the older son, once he had earned it, his father's totem became his. As the second son, Actaudin had to find his own totem. Finding a totem was important but more important was proving his courage to himself. His bravery had to be tested. This usually happened on the hunt when a young Micmac was confronted with an angry bear or moose. So far Actaudin had not been tested. Until he was, he could not enter manhood with honour. At night his mind was often filled with dreams of himself swimming powerfully out to sea and there, where the water knew no bottom, he overcame a sea lion, taming it so that it could be ridden between the islands. In other dreams he rode a whale which carried him north to the land of perpetual ice and snow where he slew great white bears with his bow and arrow.

As the sun burned higher, the fog began to lift. It rose silently, imperceptibly, revealing many islands extending far beyond the mouth of the great bay. Actaudin knew if he kept close to shore, he would be less likely to lose his way. Not that he had ever been lost. Occasionally he had taken the wrong turn but he had always been able to find his way back to camp.

It was well past noon when he finally came to the place where the grass grew into the sea and a narrow fresh water stream flowed into it. Actaudin knew of no better place for eels. He had discovered it the summer before and no one from his camp, not even Tagalak, knew exactly where it was. Actaudin wrapped two worms around the gorge and tied them in place with root twine. He dropped the line into the water. Immediately there was a jerk on the end of the line. With a strong pull he brought the squirming eel into the canoe. Using the same line, Actaudin caught another eel, then another until he had filled the birchbark pot.

"You see, Meko," Actaudin said, "my swimming has not hurt the fishing. And now that I've proved that, we'll leave the rest for tomorrow."

He stowed his fishing gear and paddled the canoe toward the shore. It was then that he thought he heard water splashing. Meko heard it too. He sat, ears tensed and pointing, in front of the canoe. He was too well-trained to bark, knowing the importance of being quiet in strange situations. Actaudin eased the canoe behind a small rocky promontory, stepped out and peered over the top of the rocks. There in the water was a white man. He was swimming easily across the channel separating the mainland from a nearby island. When he was close to the shore he stood up and began wading the short distance to the beach. To Actaudin's surprise he was not a man at all but a boy; a tall, thin boy who looked about his own age. Actaudin had never seen a white person so blond or so fair. He crept carefully along the promontory and into the woods. Meko followed and the two of them stood quietly watching the pale young man bury himself in the sand, something Actaudin often did himself. Meko too recognized the familiarity of this gesture, and after remaining still for a short time the little dog abandoned his usual caution. With his bushy tail wagging behind him, he trotted across the sand, eager to give the newcomer an exploratory sniff.

Chapter Fourteen

When I first felt that cold wet nose on my forehead, I opened my eyes and jumped up, all in one motion. I stood blinking in the sunlight, wondering if I had been dreaming. Then I began to laugh, for standing in front of me was a dog and a small dog at that. But what was a dog doing here? I thought there were only wild animals in North America: bear, moose, deer and the like. Yet this creature looked every inch a dog: he was a short-haired brown animal with pointed ears and a bushy tail that was wagging. But this was only the first of many surprises. I heard a voice.

"Meko," it said, "Meko."

The dog turned and ran toward the woods. At that moment a tall, dark-haired youth appeared from the trees and stood looking at me. I felt a wonderful surge of unexpected pleasure and excitement. Not fifty yards from me was what I had, in my first imaginings of North America, always hoped to see—an Indian; one of the inhabitants of this new land. And I could not have met one more handsome or more impressive. He was young, about my age but taller and much more strongly built. His skin was reddish brown, his eyes black, his hair dark and glossy. He stood regarding me as curiously as I did him.

When I got over my astonishment, it occurred to me that he might not be alone and that if there were others around, I might very well be in some danger. I had heard that Indians were known for their quick ambushes. Torn between wanting to meet him and my common sense which told me to return to the ship, I decided to compromise and swim back to the island, hoping he would follow me there. I had waded only a few feet into the water when he called after me.

"Wait!" he shouted.

I stopped in my tracks, wondering if I had heard correctly.

"Wait!" he repeated.

I turned around. He strode across the sand toward me and stuck out his hand.

"You stay," he said.

I took his hand and shook it dumbly, still feeling myself in some kind of a trance.

"You speak English!" I said, "How did you learn?"

He shrugged. "White trader tell me many words."

I was intrigued. Was this coastline not so deserted as my uncle thought?

"What traders?" I asked.

"Summer past. Come on ship to our village. Stay long time. They trade. We talk."

"Are they there now?"

He shook his head.

"Where is your village?"

He waved down the coast. "A day in canoe," he said.

75

"Why are you here then, if you live that far away?"

My knowledge of Indians was so slight that I did not know that fifty miles was little more than a routine hike.

"Good place for eels," he explained, pointing beyond the rocky promontory that elbowed itself into the sea. Then, as if he had decided that he had answered enough questions, he jabbed a finger at my chest and said, "Why you here?"

The question caught me off guard. I knew I shouldn't tell him about Edward's treasure or the vault he intended to build on the island. "We came on a ship," I said and let it go at that.

"To trade?"

"No, no," I said quickly, "not to trade. To build something."

He frowned. "What you build?"

This Indian was more curious and quick than any boy I had ever met. Moreover there was about him a directness which made lying to him almost impossible, so I told the truth, deliberately using difficult words so that he would not understand completely.

"We are constructing a shaft and tunnel to conceal my uncle's unlawful gains," I said.

Another frown. Then he changed the subject.

"Your name?" he asked.

"Robin."

"Robin," he repeated.

"And yours?"

"Actaudin."

It took several attempts for me to get my tongue around it.

We were still standing at the water's edge. Actaudin slipped off his moccasins and threw them onto the sand, then waded into the water.

"Come, Robin," he said, "you teach me to swim."

"Teach you to swim?" I said. "Don't you know how to swim?" With all the water around, it seemed incredible to me that I, who had grown up with only a stream nearby, could swim and he could not.

"No," he said simply, "my people not swim." Then he tapped his chest, "I do."

Although when he said those words, they were not exactly true, they soon were. It was plain to see that the reason Actaudin hadn't been able to swim was because he had not learned to relax in the water. He fought it instead, flailing and thrashing his arms and legs until he sank like a stone simply from the exertion of trying to stay afloat.

"Pretend you are going to sleep." I said to him. "Lie back and move slowly. The sea will keep you up."

Indeed the salt water was far more buoyant than the water in the Shilston stream where I learned.

After an hour or two Actaudin was floating and kicking his body across the channel. He was doing it so well that he was reluctant to leave the water long after I had had enough. My back was beginning to smart from too much sun. I knew my fair skin would be an angry red tomorrow if not sooner.

"My back hurts," I called to Actaudin, "I'm putting my clothes on."

"Wait," he said and waded ashore. He looked at my back and then headed up the beach where he disappeared behind the rocks. Within minutes he was back with a small pouch. He opened it and proceeded to smear some rank, evil-smelling liquid on my back.

"What is that?" I held my nose.

He laughed. "Bear grease. Good for skin."

"I think it works only because the smell is so bad you forget about your sunburn."

"Flies don't bite," he said.

No wonder, I thought, but said no more. Actaudin obviously considered this a favour. After he had finished he said, "We eat."

"My food is on the other side," I pointed to the sack and the pile of clothes on the opposite shore.

"Go in canoe," he said and went round the rocks again, reappearing in a canoe which he deftly manoeuvred across the channel toward my belongings. Once there he jumped out, picked up my things and paddled back toward me. All the while Meko sat alert and motionless in the bow like a small carved figurehead. As soon as the canoe was beached, however, the little dog jumped out and rolled back and forth on the sand, mostly from relief that at long last his young master was finished with the water.

"Make fire," Actaudin announced and immediately dug a small pit and set stones around it. I gathered bits of driftwood some of which seemed too beautifully shaped and coloured to burn. It wasn't long before Actaudin had a fire going, using a flint, a stone and twigs. Then he fetched a pot which like the canoe had been made from birchbark sewn together. From the pot he pulled a squirming eel which he threw to Meko. The little dog sank his teeth behind the eel's head and gradually the body stopped jerking and the dog began to eat. The second eel Actaudin skewered on a long stick which he handed to me. Then he found another stick for himself. I tried to conceal the revulsion I felt as I watched the eel I was expected to eat, writhe and twist over the flame. Actaudin grinned at my discomfort.

"Micmac not cook eels," he offered as if that would make me feel better. "I cook eels," he added proudly, obviously pleased that he was not following this particular custom.

After the eel was thoroughly browned I stripped it from the stick and began to eat, discovering in the process how hungry I was. The eel with its delicate, salty flavour turned out to be delicious. After we had eaten, Actaudin produced a pouch of berry juices, somewhat bitter but refreshing, and strings of dried moose meat. We finished the meal with the bread and cheese I had brought.

By then the sun had slipped behind the dark line of fir trees to the west, leaving only a pink blush in the sky. A bank of fog was moving slowly, eerily, landward. I yawned. The fire, the exercise and my full stomach had made me feel comfortably sleepy.

"You go back to ship?" Actaudin asked.

Up till then I had managed to forget *The Queen's Privateer*. How enjoyable it was to be free of the terrible, threatening urgency of my uncle's plans. To continue to relax on this remote beach with someone my own age for companionship was a temptation I did not want to resist. The temptation to stay was reinforced when I remembered my uncle's announcement that rum would flow aboard ship tonight. I certainly had no wish to be there when it did.

"No, I think I'll sleep here and go back to the ship tomorrow. And you?"

"I sleep here too," Actaudin said. "We talk. The white man knows much. You tell me."

"And you talk," I countered, "I want to learn about you too."

Actaudin did not answer. He had already stood up and gone into the woods to cut down fir branches for our beds. He chose only the low bushy ones which he stripped from the base of the tree with a rock hatchet. When he had enough, he arranged them into a bed on either side of the fire and placed his beaver pelt on top of one and his moosekin pelt on the other.

80

I lay down on mine, pleasantly surprised by its soft springiness and even more pleased to discover that the fur did not irritate my sunburn. The bear grease had already begun to soothe my skin. And it was true, though the blackfiles hovered above us in small clouds, they did not bite. The fog had moved into the channel, completely blocking out the island, wrapping us in a blanket. It seemed Nature had personally smiled on our friendship. We had come from such different ways of life and yet now we were enclosed in our own separate world.

Curiously enough, the fog bank was not deep and the sky above was clearly visible. We lay back and looked at the myriad stars, crowding the black night like tiny silver needlepoints.

Actaudin pointed heavenward.

"Star-people live there," he said, "it is The Land Beyond the Skies. Everything there better. People bigger. Animals too. Much food. Before she drown, my mother tell me stories about the stars."

"Your mother drowned?" The words popped unthinkingly from my mouth before I could stop them.

But Actaudin responded matter-of-factly. "My father too. Eight summers past."

So that explained why he was so determined to swim.

"My mother died when I was born," I offered. "I never knew her."

"Your father? He on ship?"

"No, he is dead." I forced myself to say the words. "He died six months ago." It was the first time since my confrontation with Edward in my grandfather's kitchen, that I had put the finality of his death into words.

Actaudin said nothing. He understood that there was nothing that could be said. For a long while we lay silently in the dark, staring into the star-filled night, the bright coals burning between us. My eyes grew heavy with sleep.

Finally Actaudin spoke.

"I tell you story of Mooin," he said.

"What's that?" I murmured drowsily.

I was able to keep my eyes open long enough to see him point to the constellation we know sometimes as the Big Dipper and at other times, as the Big Bear.

"Up there is Mooin, the Great She-Bear," he said slowly, choosing his words carefully, to get the story right. "In spring she leaves her den to journey across the sky. Chickadee, Moosebird and Robin follow. Chickadee has a cooking pot. After summer gone, star-hunters kill Mooin with bow and arrow. They eat her meat. Chickadee, Moosebird and Robin put meat in cooking pot and eat also. The bones are bare and dry but still they stay in sky all winter. In spring a new she-bear leaves her den to journey across the sky. It is the same, year after year. Always the same . . ."

Those words were the last I heard, for by the story's end I was asleep.

Chapter Fifteen

The next morning I was reminded by the abrupt clang of metal coming from the direction of the ship that I must return to the island. It was the last thing I felt like doing but I knew that my uncle would begin early to organize work crews. I did not want him to discover my absence and send Billy Boles searching for me. Nor did I want him to know about Actaudin. He would no doubt scoff at my friendship with an Indian. In his view Indians were savages and already my friendship with Actaudin was too important to be held up to his scorn.

More sounds of metal mixed with raucous, shouting voices drifted across the water. The fog still wrapped us in a white shroud, giving the sounds a strange eerie quality as if they came from no physical place. Shivering as much due to this sensation as from the early morning chill, I got up quickly.

"I must return to the island," I said, "I have work to do."

"I come," Actaudin announced.

"No," I said firmly, "it is better you stay here on the mainland."

"I come," he insisted. "I trade."

"But my uncle is very busy. He will not wish to be bothered."

"No bother. I bring beaver skin. Get axe for Taga-lak."

"Who is Tagalak?"

"My brother. He marry Wosowek in two days. I get eels for feast and," he added proudly, "I get axe!"

Now that I understood why he wanted to trade I did not see how I could refuse to help him. We had dozens of tools aboard *The Queen's Privateer*; surely my uncle would be willing to trade an axe for a beautiful beaver skin. "All right," I agreed, "you come."

Actaudin smiled. "I stay to trade. Then I go get more eels and go back to my village."

The three of us, Actaudin, Meko and I, got into the canoe and set off into the mist. We followed the island shore around until we came into the cove where *The Queen's Privateer* was anchored. It loomed out of the fog like some phantom ship.

As we came up close, I saw that members of the crew were moving equipment over the floating wharf. My uncle, I guessed, was probably in the clearing where the shaft was located. Still unnoticed, we beached the canoe. I led the way uphill through the underbrush while Actaudin followed, carrying his prized beaver skin, Meko close at his heels. The little dog was the perfect hunting companion: watchful, silent, never barking even though there were strange men around us.

My uncle stood at the top of the hill beside the shaft. The logs and canvas had been removed revealing the deep hole into which some of the men were slowly and carefully disappearing with baskets and tools. As we came closer, I could see a ladder down to the first platform. My uncle watched as Billy Boles supervised several men rigging a pulley over the shaft. The sturdiest branch of the large oak tree beside the opening extended well over the shaft. And it was from this branch that the pulley was being suspended.

My uncle heard my footstep, for he whirled about suddenly to see Actaudin following behind me. At first his expression was one of disbelief but it quickly changed to anger. Although he looked straight at Actaudin, his words were for me only.

"And who is this?" he snapped.

"This is Actaudin. He has come to trade a beaver skin for an axe."

"What do you mean, trade a beaver skin for an axe? Have you lost your wits?"

I ignored this comment. "He wants to trade with you," I repeated.

"What is this nonsense about trade? We have no time for trade." He waved his hand toward the shaft. "You know we have work to do. We cannot have savages traipsing all over the island to trade animal skins."

"He isn't a savage," I said as evenly as I could. "He's an intelligent person just like you and me."

"Is that so?" My uncle's response bore more than its usual weight of sarcasm. "So you're already an authority are you? Where did you meet him?"

"Over there," I pointed vaguely toward the mainland.

My uncle's reaction to this was one of incredulity. "Surely you were not stupid enough to go on the mainland?" he spluttered, "you could have been murdered by the savages."

"He's alone. His people do not live here," I explained, "they live in a village far down the coast."

I immediately regretted giving him this information. His eyes narrowed. "Well now, since that is the case, he will have to stay here with us," he said coolly.

Unfortunately Actaudin did not hear our words. He stood a little to one side watching the men securing the pulley. Meko sat quietly beside him, his small brown body poised for whatever action was required of him.

"What do you mean?" I asked quickly.

"What I mean is that now that he is here he will have to stay."

"But you can't do that!" I cried.

"I can and I will. If I let him go, he will return with others to trade and they will become a nuisance. I can always use another slave."

Before I could protest further he called to the first mate. "Mr. Boles, you and Wharton take this . . ." he gestured toward Actaudin, "this savage and chain him."

As the two men came towards Actaudin I shouted, "Go! Run! They're . . ."

An arm seized me around the neck and a hand was clamped over my mouth, choking off my words. My uncle had a firm hold on me. I struggled hard but against his height and superior strength, I was powerless.

Actaudin dashed across the clearing but he was too late. Billy Boles and Wharton were already on him. He struggled valiantly, kicking at his pursuers with his feet, striking out with both arms. As soon as Billy Boles reached for Actaudin, Meko grabbed hold of the first mate's leg and held on tightly. The big man swung his foot back and forth, trying to shake him loose but Meko would not let go. Enraged Billy Boles took a pistol from his belt and brought it down hard on Meko's head. There was a sharp crack of bone as the skull split. The little dog yelped once with pain and rolled over into the bushes. The blow had killed him. Even though he was obviously dead, Billy Boles gave the body several vicious swings with his boot, kicking it so hard that blood spurted from the dog's mouth.

By this time Wharton had been joined by three others and together they pinned Actaudin to a tree. Still he lunged and strained in an effort to get free.

"These savages are uncommonly strong," my uncle mused, "he will be useful, very useful indeed. Perhaps it is a good thing he happened along after all."

It was at this point that I began to hate my uncle, and to understand how cruel and merciless he could be, how totally without feeling. I struggled against him but still he held me firm. In his long arms I was as helpless as a fly caught in a spiderweb.

Chapter Sixteen

Only when Actaudin was firmly chained to a tree did my uncle let go of my arms. I turned around and faced him.

"What will you do with him?" I demanded, my voice trembling with fear and anger.

"Put him to work of course," he laughed, as if my question was the most idiotic in the world.

"But he's used to being free!" I said.

Just then Billy Boles came up behind my uncle. "If you ask me, this 'ere's one as should be put into chains with the redskin," he growled, " 'ee's nuthin' but a trouble-maker."

"There, you see?" my uncle said mockingly, "you will have to watch your step, Robin, or Mr. Boles will clap you in chains as well!"

"Mark my words," the first mate said sullenly, "this brat is nuthin' but bad luck. We got no time for the likes of 'im."

"Now, Mr. Boles," my uncle said lightly, though there

88

was an unmistakable undercurrent of malice in his voice, "I am sure my nephew realizes how important it is that he work with us, not against us. Don't you, Robin? And now," he continued smoothly, "I think it is time the first crew was in the tunnel. Our new captive will go with the second string."

The first mate grunted and lumbered off toward the ship.

I still had to find out what would happen to Actaudin. "Will you let him go? I mean afterwards? When the work here is finished?"

My uncle started toward the shaft. I followed him.

"Well, will you?" I persisted.

He did not even bother to turn around but stood, hands on hips, staring into the pit. And though he spoke, it was in that impatient, offhand way that indicated how little he cared about how I felt. "Don't make a nuisance of yourself, Robin, or I shall have to follow Mr. Boles' advice and clap you into chains. Now I suggest you make yourself useful. I want the angle of the tunnel and where it surfaces at the cove checked and rechecked. Immediately. So you had better get the measuring instruments ready."

I had been defeated. The helplessness I felt was total. I looked at Actaudin. He was leaning against the tree. They had chained both his arms and legs to the thick trunk. Even so, he held his head up. I went to him.

"I'm sorry," I said, "I didn't know this would happen. It was stupid of me. I should have come alone."

Actaudin made no response. He looked through me rather than at me, his eyes dark and unfathomable.

"You don't think I wanted this to happen, do you?" I cried.

Silence.

"Listen carefully," I said, keeping my voice low so the

crew members would not hear, "this island is very important to my uncle. When we finish here, he might let you go back to your people."

Still no answer. Only that steady gaze, focussed somewhere beyond me. Didn't he understand what I was saying?

"And if my uncle won't let you go," I whispered fiercely into his ear, "I will set you free! I promise!"

It was then Actaudin turned toward me. "You make trap for me. Not my friend. White people lie." He spat these words into my face.

"That's not true," I said. "There was no trap. I told no lies."

But he would say no more. He had said what he thought and that was that. I stood there rejected and miserable. Yet I couldn't blame Actaudin. He could not have known how much I hated my uncle's treachery.

I turned toward him once more. "You may not believe me," I whispered, my voice trembling, "but I will set you free! You'll see!"

I could not bear to look at his hostile eyes any longer and ran toward the ship, tripping over the brown body of Meko lying on the ground not far from the tree to which Actaudin was chained. I had forgotten about the little dog. He ought at least to have a decent burial. Carefully I lifted the limp body in my arms and carried him toward the shore away from the clearing. When I found a spot where the earth was loose and easily removed, I laid him down and returned to the ship for a shovel.

By that time the sun had risen overhead, burning off the fog that had enclosed us in our ghostly world. Now I saw clearly across the water. Billy Boles was at the oars of a Jolly-boat, rowing toward the mainland, Actaudin's canoe in tow. I could guess what he was doing. He was taking the canoe down the coast where it would be overturned close to shore, scattering the eel pots and skin pouches on the sandy bottom. This ruse was obviously for the day when Actaudin's people came looking for him. They would find the empty canoe which by then would have drifted nearer their village. Naturally they would assume Actaudin had drowned and would look for him no more. As far as his people were concerned, Actaudin was dead.

When I found a shovel, I returned to the island, dug a deep hole, placed Meko inside and covered him over. By the time I had finished this sad task, I could scarcely see. The tears would no longer be held back. The loss of my father, Actaudin and Meko all came together under the heavy spectre of my uncle, and I sat by the grave and wept.

Chapter Seventeen

After his capture I was seldom able to see Actaudin, except at night. Because of his obvious strength he had been put to work in the underground tunnel whereas my uncle saw to it that I was kept busy aboveground. So far we had no need of the pump. Since coming to the island not one drop of rain had fallen, an unusual occurrence and one that worked in my uncle's favour. He insisted that I keep rechecking my father's calculations which I had already done several times before but which had to be done over and over in order to satisfy his increasing demands. With every day that passed he became more and more obsessed with the idea something might go wrong with the project.

In addition, I was required to build stone triangles which my father had designed as markers for relocating the main shaft and tunnel. These were important for the day when Edward returned for his treasure. I was also expected to remove buckets from the pulley, replacing those filled with dirt with empty ones. The buckets of dirt brought up from the bottom of the shaft where the tunnel was being dug were emptied onto a wagon drawn by eight slaves hitched to it like horses. Taken downhill and loaded onto rafts manned by black men chained to the oars like galley slaves, the dirt was rowed out of the cove and dumped into the sea. This was a vital part of the plan. When the shaft and tunnel were completed there must be no tell-tale signs such as piles of dirt to indicate the presence of tunnelling below. Sometimes I was assigned the task of hauling stones from the beach for placing in the tunnel to prevent its collapse after the hard-packed earth had been removed and the sea allowed in.

Through all this activity, the slaves, Actaudin among them, were driven with whips and beaten with sticks to force them to work long after they were exhausted. Even the slave who had tried to jump ship on the voyage was expected to be useful, being chained with others to one of the rafts. The slaves were treated no better than dogs. At night they were chained to the trees surrounding the clearing. Each was given a ragged blanket on which to find some comfort, a bowl of thin soup and a chunk of bread. Nothing was done to alleviate the raw sores at their ankles or the whip wounds on their backs.

I had expected that as ship's surgeon, Powderlegs might do something to ease the slaves' wretched condition but he did not. Perhaps Edward had ordered him not to but I think he was simply too lazy and indifferent to bother. However, when I went to the dispensary, he did let me take jars of salve which worked wonders on skin tortured by sores and whip wounds. I developed the habit of going round to the slaves after dark when the crewmen were back on ship. Some of them would not allow me near them and pushed me roughly away. They had reached the point where cruelty was easier to bear than kindness. Others let me tend their wounds and apply the salve.

While I went about these duties I sensed Actaudin's dark eyes watching me but whenever I went near him, he assumed the same see-through stare. I began to understand that this anger which he directed toward me was his way of holding onto his dignity. Most of the other slaves had long since lost their pride—it had been beaten out of them—but Actaudin held tenaciously to his. It was evident in his eyes and in the way he moved. Even though he had become much thinner, his face gaunt and his hair matted with dirt, he continued to carry himself in his purposeful, confident way.

Until the day he rebelled. It was morning and the work crews were being lined up in the clearing beside the pit. When his turn came to climb down the ladder, he refused. He had reached a point of desperation where the rebellion that boiled inside him could no longer be suppressed. Of course it was a mistake. As soon as Billy Boles realized that Actaudin had no intention of entering the shaft, he brought his whip down on his back in a succession of brutal blows that kept coming until Actaudin was forced to his knees, his back a mass of raw, bleeding welts.

From where I stood I could see that the edges of skin were shredded and torn. Anger and disgust welled up in me. I wanted to wrench the whip from that bullying monster. But I knew better. I was slowly, painfully, learning the wisdom of self control. It would be a pointless exercise to interfere. The first mate would only turn on me and afterwards I might not be in a condition to help Actaudin. Better to swallow my anger and wait until I could be of real help. To make matters worse Actaudin was forced to work in the tunnel the rest of the day even though he could hardly crawl into the pit.

94

That evening when I found him in the clearing, his wounds were tightly packed with dirt. He was too exhausted even to eat the crust of bread or drink the cold soup left beside his blanket. He lay, his knees pulled up to his chest, I suppose to ease his pain, his eyes vacant and staring. When I knelt beside him with a jug of sea water I had brought with me, he gave no sign he even noticed me which wasn't unusual except this time his eyes were empty of anger. Anger, his final weapon, had been stripped away.

"I'll fix your back," I said. He made no response. I could do what I wanted. It no longer mattered.

It took several jugfuls to wash away the mud. At least the dirt had prevented black flies from infesting his bleeding stripes. Though the sea water stung, Actaudin made no sound as I worked. At last the wounds were clean and I spread salve thickly on top.

"It will feel better tomorrow," I said.

To my surprise he answered me, the first words he had spoken since his capture.

"I die here," he said, "my people not come."

"You won't die," I said, though I had a terrible fear that what he said was true. All this time he had been living on the hope that his people, probably his brother Tagalak, would come looking for him and somehow manage to free him. He did not know that his canoe had been set adrift.

"I die," he repeated in that definite way, "I see my people no more."

I had to find a way of distracting him, of giving him hope.

"Look at the stars," I said, "there are so many of them tonight."

It was true. The night sky was ablaze with stars.

He turned his eyes upward. "The star-people see me. Last night I dream. Mooin says she come," he said.

"And will she?"

"She come but I cannot follow now."

"Can Mooin help you?"

"Only if I free. I must go to her. I die. Then I see her in The Land Beyond the Skies."

He found hope in his belief that he would join the star-people. If he died he would go to The Land Beyond the Skies where everything was perfect and good. Even if it meant he had to die to go, that land was far better than enduring this cruel existence.

I said no more that night. Nor did I make promises I was not sure I could keep. But I was determined to help Actaudin escape. And I would do it as soon as possible while he still had the strength to get back to his people.

But was it possible? The only way to open the manacle chaining him to this island was to use the master key that was used to open all the manacles. It was suspended from Billy Boles' belt by a long loop of wire so that he could use it without having to remove it. I had seen him use it many times. How could I hope to get it off? The seeming impossibility of this task depressed me because I could see no other alternative.

To talk to my uncle about freeing Actaudin was useless. I had tried that and failed. If I were to approach him again he might guess my intention and put me under close watch which would prevent me from doing anything. As it stood now, I could move about much as I pleased. The more I thought about it, the clearer it became that Actaudin would never be allowed to return to his people, even after the tunnel was finished. He knew about the shaft and tunnelling and therefore would probably tell his people where it was. My uncle would never take that chance. I did not know what Edward intended to do with the slaves when their work on the island was finished, but I was certain his plans did not include freedom. In any case, because of the dangerous work and the way they were driven, it was possible that none of the slaves, including Actaudin, would survive the summer.

Chapter Eighteen

For five days I waited and watched, trying to think of some way to get hold of the key. Then one night as I started to go on my rounds of the slaves, I remembered I was down to my last jar of salve and it was half empty. I decided to fetch another from the dispensary before leaving the ship.

The dispensary was below deck just at the bottom of a dimly lit companionway. I climbed down warily. I had twisted my ankle on the bottom step one day and that had taught me to be careful. Had I come charging down the stairs at full speed in my old style, I might never have discovered a way of getting Billy Boles' key. Part way down the steps I realized the door was ajar. Billy Boles and Powderlegs were talking quietly inside. I flattened myself against the wall, straining to hear.

"That young fella's been coming in here nights," I heard Powderlegs say, "askin' fer salve. I believe he's been fixin' up them slaves."

Billy Boles grunted. " 'Ee's meddlin'. Always meddlin'. The Cap'n shoulda left that whelp back where 'ee was. 'Ee's nuthin' but trouble."

They were talking about me! I inched as near to the door as I could without being seen. I was so close I could hear Powderlegs set down a bottle after he had taken a drink. Both he and Billy Boles were obviously well into the rum. When he spoke, Powderlegs slurred his words together as he had the day he told me about Vigo Bay.

"He ain't so bad. Jest got a kind heart he has. You hafta admit, Billy, them slaves is a miserable lot. Can't stand the sight of 'em myself. A bit o'salve on them wounds won't hurt, now will it?"

"You don't know nuthin' about it," Billy growled in return, his voice becoming more heavy and coarse with drink. "You got to treat 'em rough. Else they won't work. Jest lay down on the job. Whipped that savage real good a while back cause 'ee wouldn't move. Afterwards, 'ee worked real good."

Though I could not see him I knew Billy Boles' mouth was shaped into a cruel grin as he remembered how he had beaten Actaudin into submission.

There was a long interval of silent drinking and then Billy Boles' ominous voice again, "Y'know, I been thinkin'," he said, "we may 'aft to get tough with the Cap'n afore we're through."

"Now, now. The Cap'n's a reasonable man. He ain't made no mistakes yet."

"Not with us watchin' 'im 'ee ain't. 'Ee knows we keeps a close eye on 'im. We's onto 'im. Soon as we leaves this island, 'ee's goin to dump them slaves overboard. Course, they's a scurvy lot anyway. 'Alf starved with the rations cut back so far. They'll be no good fer nuthin' by the time's we's done. We knows 'is plans fer the crew too. Soon as they gits this ship close 'nough to

Boston, ee'll explode 'er and scuttle the whole works. The three of us'll git ashore but the crew'll go down in the night and never know what 'appened. Now I says a man who does that to 'is crew, 'ee's not to be trusted. We gotta keep an eye on 'im."

The stark horror of Billy Boles' statement chilled me to the bone. I had already decided that my uncle had no intention of freeing the slaves who survived the summer but it had never occurred to me that he would throw them overboard in cold blood. And certainly it had never occurred to me that he would plan to kill his crew! Was I also included in his plans? Would he make sure I went down with the scuttled ship? I did not want to believe that Edward would murder his own brother's son, but I could not deny the facts. I not only knew about the treasure, I knew about the floodgate and how to use the pump so that I was much more dangerous to him than his crew. The sudden horrifying realization that my life too was probably in jeopardy filled me with such terror that my knees began to shake and I had to crouch down to keep from toppling over and giving myself away. I heard Powderlegs speak.

"All I know is the Cap'ns been good to me. Saved me life he did and a man can't do more than that, now can he?"

Billy Boles did not answer. His mind was still on his own survival. It was clear that he feared my uncle. Although his brain was dulled by the rum, he suspected he was tolerated only to do Edward's dirty work for him and because *The Queen's Privateer* could not be sailed single-handedly. He had begun to fear that once the treasure was in the ground and they had left the island, my uncle would get rid of him too. Obviously Billy Boles was trying to win Powderlegs over to share his distrust of my uncle, but the "monkey," cripple that he was, was

100

too clever for that. His survival depended on a man stronger than himself and in any struggle between my uncle and Billy Boles my uncle was sure to win. Most of the time he balanced himself between the first mate and the Cap'n but he left no doubt which man he would choose if it ever came to making a choice.

Sensing this, Billy Boles changed the subject. "One thing sure. That young whelp 'as got to go. I'll do it me-self one of these days."

"Now, Billy, no need to be hasty," Powderlegs said, "no need to be hasty. The Cap'n has plans fer the boy. He has to man the pump."

"Pump or not. I ain't cuttin' in fer that whelp. Too smart 'ee is. I got plans fer 'im, I 'ave."

With the awful picture of Billy Boles looming over me, terror gripped me so tightly I felt light-headed and faint. To this day I do not know how I managed to remain out-side that door when my impulse was to bolt up the stairs, plunge into the water and swim far, far away. Such was my panic at that moment. But I knew my survival de-pended on out-thinking my uncle. As I crouched against the wall, as much for support as for stealth, I began mak-ing a plan of my own.

I would leave the island tonight. While Billy Boles was sleeping I would somehow sneak the master key off his belt, free Actaudin and escape with him to his people.

Suddenly there was a scrape of boots across the dis-pensary floor. For one panic-stricken moment I thought Billy Boles was heading for the door, but then I heard the sound of the sea chest being opened and knew then he was after more rum. The sound of a bottle being opened confirmed it. Good. My plan was more likely to be successful if Billy Boles and Powderlegs were both thoroughly drunk. With them in a stupor, I stood a much better chance of getting the key off the first mate's belt

101

without waking him. But it would take hours of drinking for them to reach this state. I could not stay that long in the companionway. I would have to go back to my cabin. I got to my feet, and putting my full weight on the rail, I managed to climb the stairs without them squeaking and crept across deck, down to my cabin.

The first thing I did was to stuff my pockets with raisins and a chunk of stale bread to sustain Actaudin and myself on our flight. Then I stretched out on my bunk to wait. I was too excited and scared to sleep but I knew I must at least try to rest. Actaudin's village was far away; there would be miles of wilderness to cross and we would have to travel quickly to put a long distance between ourselves and my uncle, before daybreak alerted him to our escape.

So I lay on my bunk, concentrating on the sounds of *The Queen's Privateer*, trying desperately to stay calm. The ship was never quiet. It rose and fell, sighing with each swell, and there was always the intermittent creaking of its wooden bones. Except for these sounds, there was silence. The crew had long since fallen asleep.

At last when the moon was directly over the ship, I stepped out into the narrow passage and, groping my way carefully to avoid tripping over unseen objects, made my way back to the dispensary.

The door was still ajar, but there were no voices. Powderlegs and Billy Boles were both asleep. I slipped past the door and into the room. There was about two inches of candle still burning. Billy Boles lay on his back, spread-eagled across the upper bunk and Powderlegs lay on the other. Both men were in a deep slumber: Billy Boles, snoring, his mouth agape, looked fierce, even in sleep. As I approached him, one slow, cautious step at a time, I had the awful premonition that his eyes would suddenly open and he would leap up and seize me. Even the dead so terrify us. My hands shook as I undid his belt buckle and slid off the wire loop. Once the master key was in my hand I had to restrain myself to keep from dashing out the door. I forced myself to move slowly and carefully. Leaving the buckle open, I slipped back through the door, and up the companionway to the deck. It was only after I had crossed the wharf platforms to the shore that I broke into a frenzied run.

Actaudin was asleep, but as soon as I touched the ankle lock with the key, his eyes opened. He did not move right away. It took him a few moments to realize that I was actually unlocking the manacle. The iron band snapped open.

"You are free," I whispered, "you can go back to your people now. But we must hurry!" Actaudin's face broke into a smile, the first I had seen since my uncle took him prisoner. He staggered to his feet. After the heavy ankle chain he had been dragging around for weeks, his leg felt weak and feather light.

"You come," he said, as he cautiously swung his leg back and forth.

"Yes, I come. But we must hurry," I repeated urgently. "We must get as far away as possible before sunrise."

The moon was high and bright: I guessed it to be midnight. If we were lucky we had nearly six hours before the crew stirred.

Some of the slaves chained in the clearing were awakened by our whispers. They began to move about restlessly, their manacles clinking. In that moment I knew that before I could escape I must also free the slaves. With any luck maybe some of them would get off the island. Intoxicated by the power of one small key, I unlocked the ankle chain of the slave nearest Actaudin.

"Go!" I whispered, pointing to the mainland. "Go!"

As he stumbled away, I went to the next, unlocked his manacle and repeated the same directions. I got no further than the fifth lock when I heard Billy Boles' savage roar behind me and knew that I was doomed. The last thing I saw was Actaudin's figure disappearing into the bushes as a terrrible pain split my head and I fell into blackness.

Chapter Nineteen

It took Actaudin three days to reach his village. He kept moving that first night, to put the island and all its terror as far behind him as possible and to keep warm. He had seldom travelled at night before and took great pleasure in the night creatures: the bats swooping, the owls screeching, the tiny deer mice scuttling through the leaves to stay ahead of the wolverine's lightning thrust. He felt safe in the forest among animals he trusted and understood. How wonderful to be free at last, to have escaped the white man's dreadful shadow. If he had not understood the danger in trusting them before, he certainly did now.

At noon he was forced to rest. He stopped in a sun-warmed clearing where the raspberries had ripened. After eating every berry he could find, he lay down and slept, the medicine-sun warm on his whip-scarred back.

The moon was high when at last he came to his village. His heart leapt at the sight of the wigwams, the smoke curling upward from their cone-shaped roofs. He recognized Tagalak's new wigwam by the mark over the entrance. He went over to it, lifted the flap, stooped and entered. His brother and his new wife sat beside the fire. When Actaudin appeared in front of them, looking thin and haggard, Wosowek drew back in fear.

"Aieeee! I see Actaudin's ghost!"

Actaudin laughed.

Even Tagalak approached him cautiously. "Is it really you, little brother?" he asked.

"Have I changed so much? Yes, it's me."

Tagalak embraced him warmly. "Wosowek, this is no ghost. This is my little brother. We gave you up for dead," he said gravely, "when we saw the canoe drift to shore empty. We thought you had drowned."

Wosowek noticed the whip marks.

"What happened to your back?" she asked.

"The white man whipped me," Actaudin said.

"You have been with the white man all this time?"

"Yes. They captured me and made me work in a deep hole in the ground."

"Deep in the ground? In The Land of Souls?" Tagalak asked wonderingly. He looked at Actaudin as if he might be a ghost after all.

Wosowek chose this time to speak. "There will be time for stories later. Right now I shall fetch Malwalbe to see to these wounds."

She went out, returning soon with the old medicine man. Malwalbe examined the whip marks carefully, then put balsam of the fir tree over Actaudin's back to speed its healing. Afterwards he gave him a drink of warm broth into which he had crushed mint leaves.

"You are fortunate, it is healing well," the old man said. "All you need now is good food to rebuild your limbs and make you strong again."

106

"We shall have a special feast tonight to honour my brother's return," Tagalak said joyfully, "then he can eat all he wants."

That night the fire outside Alsoosit's wigwam had never seemed brighter. Not only did Actaudin join the men around the fire but he was given a special place at Alsoosit's right hand. It was the first time he had ever been so honoured. After they had feasted, wiping their hands carefully on their hair, Alsoosit spoke, his voice quavering with age and emotion.

"When our son, Actaudin, went away, we thought he had drowned. We had a death-feast to help speed his journey through The Land of Souls to The Land Beyond the Skies where his mother and father now dwell. But he is not dead as we had thought. He has come back to us and we feast again, this time to celebrate his life."

During this speech Actaudin kept his eyes averted. He did not dare look at the others for fear of smiling his happiness and spoiling the solemnity of the occasion.

"He has much to tell us of his journey," Alsoosit continued. "We shall listen closely as he speaks to us."

This was the moment Actaudin had been waiting for; now he could tell them that the white man was not so easily trusted as some of them, including himself, had thought.

"A day's journey by canoe from here is an island with white men on it. It was close to there that I went to fish for eels. There I met a white boy named Robin. We talked and ate together. In the morning I crossed to the island with him so I could trade a beaver skin. On the island were many white men and black men we have never seen before. The white men make slaves of the black men."

There was a murmur of disapproval among the men. There were other Indian tribes far away who were said to make slaves of captives but they did not approve of it themselves.

"The white men are evil and not to be trusted," Actaudin continued. "They captured me, killed my dog Meko, and bound my feet in iron so that I could not walk properly. They made a slave of me. The white men have many tools and weapons. They have dug a huge hole in the ground with a pathway deep inside that runs toward the sea."

"Why do they do that?" Alsoosit asked.

"I do not know," Actaudin said, "but they have many goods, weapons and tools and I think they want to hide them."

"They beat you to make you do their work for them," Alsoosit said.

"Yes. They made me work underground in The Land of Souls."

There was a shocked silence among the men, then they began to speak angrily to one another.

Tagalak's voice rose loudly above the others. "We must go to the island," he said, "and teach those white men a lesson!"

"Yes. Yes. We must do that!" agreed the man who sat beside Tagalak. Actaudin recognized him as Wosowek's father.

"No!" Actaudin said sharply. It had never occurred to him that his people would seek revenge against his captors. At first he was unprepared to deal with the idea.

"There are so many of them. We would all be killed," he said.

"We do not fear them," Tagalak retorted scornfully, "we can join with others of our tribe."

Actaudin knew he had made a mistake in suggesting that the white man could overpower them. He must think of some way to prevent Tagalak from persuading the others that revenge was necessary. With their weapons the white man could kill all of them. He looked at the men arguing around the campfire.

"It would not be good for all of us to go to the island," Actaudin spoke slowly, choosing his words carefully. "It is haunted by the ghosts of the dead. As I told you the white men have dug deep within the ground. They have entered The Land of Souls and the ghosts of our people walk the ground looking for us. They come from underground paths calling our names. If we all go to the island, we will disturb the dead and they will come for us."

For a while no one said anything, not even Tagalak. No one wanted to speak of meeting the dead or of entering their land. For each, death would come soon enough. Actaudin knew they would question him no more. It was taboo to talk about The Land of Souls, of those people who had died but had not yet made their journey from their graves to The Land Beyond the Skies.

Then Actaudin spoke again. "I must go back to the island by myself."

At once there were protests from everyone around the campfire.

"Why must you return to the island?" asked Alsoosit, his voice rising above the others.

"Because of Robin, the boy I told you about. When I was first captured I thought he had set a trap for me and I wouldn't speak to him. But then he set me free. There was a tool to open the iron band. He got it for me while the white men slept," Actaudin explained.

"Then he was your friend," Alsoosit said.

"Yes," Actaudin said simply, "he was my friend. And when he saved me from The Land of the Souls he put himself in great danger. After he freed me he began to free the black men and he did not see the man with the whip come up behind him. If Robin is still alive he will be

109

a prisoner like I was. The evil one will have put him chains for freeing us. He freed me, and now I must return to free him."

"We will all go to free him," exclaimed Tagalak.

"No," said Actaudin sharply. "It will be safer for me to go alone. One person can move around without being seen more safely than many can," he explained earnestly. "And one person is not as likely to disturb the ghosts of our people."

"Actaudin is right," said Alsoosit. "We shall not seek out the white man. We will not disturb the dead. And it will be safer for Actaudin to return alone to the island to free his friend. As soon as he has regained his strength he will go." Then Alsoosit handed the pipe to Actaudin. "It is good to find wisdom in one so young. It comforts me to know our people will not lack for a strong leader."

Actaudin took his pipe. This time he did not try to suppress the joy that welled up in his chest. The agony of captivity, the painful assault on his back seemed worth this precious moment when he smoked with his people.

During the next few days, Actaudin stayed close to his village. He slept and ate, fished, dug clams and swam in the ocean. By the week of the big storm he had almost regained the strength he had lost while he was a prisoner and he was eager to be on his way to rescue Robin.

But the first autumn rains swept into the village with all of Kesulk's fury. Roaring waves slammed against the beach. Winds ripped through birchbark doorways. Fires smoked and sizzled as rain trickled into the wigwams through the smoke holes. Actaudin and his people waited out the storm inside their wigwams. The waiting made Actaudin restless. At night he could not sleep but tossed fitfully on his bed. One night Alsoosit spoke through the darkness of the wigwam, the darkness shared with Atkegwee who was snoring peacefully on her bed despite the wind shrieking outside.

"You are troubled about your friend," Alsoosit said. Even when competing with the wind, he spoke with great authority.

"Yes."

"You fear he might lose himself in The Land of Souls?"

"Yes," Actaudin agreed. Ever since he had come to live in Alsoosit's wigwam, he had been astonished by the old man's wisdom. Alsoosit understood many things without ever having been told.

"When he saved you from The Land of Souls," Alsoosit went on, "he took great risk to himself."

"Yes," Actaudin agreed. "As soon as the storm ends I must leave for the island."

Alsoosit knew it was more than proving his friendship to the white boy. It was time for Actaudin to prove his courage.

Neither spoke again that night. But one morning two days later, after the storm had passed, Alsoosit arose and saw Actaudin's bed was empty and that one of his canoes was gone.

By the time Alsoosit discovered this, Actaudin was already several miles up the coast. In his canoe he had his stone hatchet, two weeks' supply of dried moose meat and beaver skins. He would hide the canoe two miles down the coast, swim the channel at night, and with the thick forest to shelter him, he would watch the clearing. If Robin was alive, he would try to set him free. He understood very clearly the risk he was taking. The white man had many weapons that could kill him with one flash of fire. But he had to take that risk.

111

Chapter Twenty

"Ee's comin' to. Didn't hit 'im hard enough."

I lay on the floor of my uncle's cabin. I had opened my eyes briefly to see where I was, then quickly closed them again. But Billy Boles had caught their flutter.

"For your sake, Mr. Boles," I heard my uncle's haughty voice, "I hope you only tapped him."

"Ee's nuthin' but trouble," muttered the first mate, "shoulda got rid of 'im long ago."

"How many times have I told you we need my nephew to assemble the pump?" my uncle snapped, impatient with Billy Boles' thickheadedness. "Did you get all the slaves?"

"Was like roundin' up worms. They was so confused they got nowheres. I found 'em crawlin' in the bushes."

Billy Boles' blow must have dazed me badly because it was only then that I remembered freeing Actaudin and some of the slaves.

My uncle tapped his desk, "Did you get the savage?"

"Not a trace of 'im," Billy Boles admitted sullenly.

He had escaped! I had at least accomplished that.

"You should have gone after him and left the others. If he gets back to his people, we'll have savages all over the island."

"Now, Cap'n," Powderlegs intervened, "I wouldn't say that. He may never git to the others. If he does, and they's stupid enough to come here, we got pistols and cannons. Bows n' arrows is toys to us. 'Sides we only got coupla weeks afore we's through and 'til then we can post a sentry. We got enough crew fer that."

This seemed to pacify my uncle. He walked over to where I lay. I felt the toe of his boot against my jacket. I kept my eyes closed, unwilling to give any sign that I was conscious. Besides, I was not at all sure I could stand, or for that matter, sit. My head throbbed unbearably. The only remedy was to lie absolutely still.

"As for my nephew," I heard Edward say, "we shall put him in the savage's chains. Since he is so fond of slaves he can become one himself." He laughed unpleasantly, knowing full well I heard every word.

"Why bother? The sooner 'ees dead, the better," Billy Boles insisted.

"Mr. Boles," my uncle said, "it's a pity you are so pig-headed, though I must say it works to our advantage sometimes. Everyone has his use. Even you. Right now yours is to follow my orders, which includes keeping my nephew alive until he has outlived his usefulness, which is to assemble the pump and show me how to work it."

"Don't see why we need a pump," the first mate argued. "Shaft's as dry as a bone. Anyways, I thought we was usin' water to guard the gold."

"We are," snapped my uncle impatiently. "Once the treasure is in place we'll flood the tunnel and the bottom part of the shaft. Surely," he continued sarcastically,

113

"even you realize we'll need the pump to empty out this water when we come back to get the treasure. And to do that we'll have to know how to assemble and use it, won't we? In any case, if it rains and water gets into the vault before we put the treasure in place, we'll want to pump it out. That would also give us proof that the pump actually works."

"Why can't you study yer brother's plans and work the pump yerself?" Billy Boles asked petulantly, refusing to give up the argument.

"Now, Billy," Powderlegs said, "the Cap'n's a man of the sea, not an inventor. Once the boy gets the thing together, the Cap'n'll know how it works. After that, you'll have your way."

The idea of having his way with me prompted the first mate to give me a kick. I cried out from the sharpness of the pain.

"That's enough, you fool," my uncle exclaimed, "he's to be kept alive. He can't assemble the pump dead, can he? Mark my words, Mr. Boles, if you kill my nephew before he does his job, I'll see you swing from the highest oak tree on this island."

I heard Billy Boles mutter under his breath. Powderlegs again intervened. "Why not leave the boy here fer the night? We could tie him to a chair."

I knew this was no kindness to me; he was as cruel as the others. He simply saw the wisdom of keeping me away from Billy Boles until the first mate got over his anger because I had stolen his key. At the same time I would be under the watchful eye of my uncle. Billy Boles lifted me up and threw me onto the chair. Then he fetched some rope and tied me to it. During all this I kept my body limp, pretending unconsciousness. It seemed the only thing to do. I was as good as dead anyway. I must admit that I was sorry I had freed the slaves. If I had fled with Actaudin, I would be safe now. Finally I could stay quiet no longer and cried miserably until my uncle crossed the room and cuffed me on the face.

Eventually I fell into an exhausted sleep. Sometime later I was awakened by Powderlegs' voice. He was perched on my uncle's desk, twirling one of his crutches as he spoke to Edward who was tipped back in his chair, a silver wine goblet in his hand.

"It's true, Cap'n, we was into the rum but not as much as you might think. Leastways not me. I saw that young whelp sneak otta the room with the key. Billy was sleepin' awful deep. I kept pokin' him with my crutch 'til he woke up. When I told him what happened he was so mad, roarin' and cursin', I's afraid he'd kill the boy so I hightailed it after him so's he wouldn't do him in."

"A good thing you used your head," my uncle said. "Boles tries to kill everything that gets in his way. If he's not careful he'll soon be in *our* way. Once we're done here, we may have to get rid of him with the rest of the crew. Otherwise he'll cause us no end of trouble. Don't you agree?"

Powderlegs slapped his leg stumps. "Yes siree. It's lookin' that way. Billy could give us away. 'Sides, I never could divide by three!"

My uncle thought this remark uproariously funny, yet I had no doubt that in the end he would find himself unable to divide, even by two.

After Powderlegs left, I became even more convinced that my uncle would never divide the treasure with anyone. No sooner had the "monkey" gone than Edward bolted the door and crossed to the panelled wall behind his desk. Lighting a taper he slid one of the panels aside, revealing a room inside. I could just make out the outline of a chest. So my earlier guess had been right! The trea-

115

sure was hidden in my uncle's cabin. Setting the candle down, my uncle opened the chest. I watched fascinated as he picked up handfuls of coins, held them up and then let them drop back into the chest. As I drifted again into sleep, he was still moving from chest to chest.

Chapter Twenty-One

I am convinced that I survived the following days only because of my stubborn will to live. Every day I and the other slaves to whom I was chained risked death. For the descent down the shaft our heavy ankle manacles were removed and lighter wrist bands snapped on. Otherwise it would have been impossible for us to move up and down the ladders. Eight of us were chained together in each string. If one of us was to slip, the entire lot slipped with him. And on my first morning in chains, that is exactly what happened. The first string was entering the shaft when the sixth man in line slipped. I shall never forget the look of shock and terror on the faces of the last two men on the ladder as they were jerked from the edge of the shaft and plunged downward. I covered my ears so that I would not hear their agonized screams, but I heard them nonetheless. When the bodies were brought up one by one by the pulley rigged to the big oak tree, I saw that only five were dead; the other three had been badly injured.

"Mr. Boles, take these corpses to the cove and dispose of them," my uncle said briskly, his cold features unmoved by the horror of the accident. "Use one of the rafts."

Soon after I heard three pistol shots. The three slaves who had survived the fall had been shot like work-horses which have outlived their usefulness. I knew that like the slaves who had died over the summer either from suffocation, malnutrition or from being beaten to death, their bodies would be weighted with stones and dropped into the sea. I had no idea how many slaves had been disposed of in this way; only that of all those who had made the chilly passage across the Atlantic, fewer than half were still alive. This suited my uncle's purpose, for he had got the digging he wanted out of them before they died. With the work on the tunnel nearly done he needed only half as many men as before, and the fewer slaves who lived the fewer there would be to get rid of when the job was done. My uncle had learned much about the uses of the sea. Not only would it guard his wealth, but it concealed a multitude of sins as well.

When it came my turn to descend the ladder with the seven slaves in my string, I found myself unable to move and was jolted to the dust by the chain being pulled taut. I was certain I would never be able to climb down the ladder. Seeing my terror, Edward unlocked my chain with the key he had commandeered while the first mate went about the grisly burial.

"You may go down by yourself this time, to get used to it," he said, "and be manacled at the bottom."

This was no kindness on my uncle's part; he needed me alive. Down I went, following the others into that deep hole, the daylight disappearing with each platform, until the only light came from the lanterns flickering over the earth walls. I did not stop until I had gone past the vault

119

and was at the tunnel's entrance. There I was again manacled to the slaves in my string.

By this time the tunnel extended far underground. We
were now digging the section of the tunnel between the
airshaft and that part of the tunnel where the floodgate
was to be put in position and where we would connect
with the crews digging towards us from the beach. The
airshaft had been dug down from the surface well along
the tunnel construction to provide some ventilation, but
it had been constructed only after nearly a third of the
slaves had died from suffocation. Even with the airshaft
behind us, there was never enough air and our lungs constantly ached with the effort to breathe in the stale air.

Further and further we dug, upward toward the spot
where the tunnel would intercept another narrow shaft
dug down from the surface. Here the floodgate of heavy
timbers would be lowered down to us to put in place. Although my reason told me that until the tunnel was connected to its beach section and the floodgate removed,
our part of the tunnel would remain dry, still I could not
rid my mind of the awful vision of sea water breaking
through, washing us back into the main shaft like so
many drowned rats.

The tunnel was so narrow that we had to crawl, one at
a time, into it, each man on the heels of the one in front.
Only one man could dig at a time. Hard against the tunnel's end, hemmed in by the men behind, elbows pressed
against our sides by the cold dark walls, each of us took
his turn scraping away his share of packed earth with a
metal scoop, dumping his contribution into a wooden
tray. The others in the string then slid the tray full of
dirt back into the tunnel and another crew took it to the
surface. All of this was done in total blackness; we were
pitiful moles scrabbling blindly after one another. The
most we could endure was five minutes—and they

120

seemed an eternity—before we began heaving and panting in our desperate gulpings for whatever fresh air was left in our small space. The very walls seemed to close in on us. It always reached this stage before our lead line pulled us back into the airshaft opening where we gulped enough air to continue digging. This routine of getting our breath every five minutes so we could resume digging continued until we could scarcely lift a hand. At that point we were pulled backward past the airshaft opening where we gulped enough air for the long pull back along the tunnel and into the main shaft. There we stumbled about on the bottom platform, gasping and panting in an effort to force enough air into our lungs to make our chests stop heaving. While we rested, another string crawled in to repeat the performance. When they came out, we went back in. Each time I went in, I was certain I would not come out alive.

Day after day we followed this pattern, always in the same way, so that a sort of rhythm was established. And because of this repetition we ceased to think or feel. I forgot about my father, my grandfather and Actaudin. I forgot what I had once been. I became like an animal, surviving on instinct and only in that way did I endure the horror. I remember on the first day in the pit being surprised that the slaves took no notice of me, but for them life held no more surprises. After a few days of bondage I understood. I was not even surprised when two days before the outbreak of the big storm, we reached the opening of the floodgate access shaft. After much struggling we managed to put the floodgate into position. From sounds on the opposite side of the gate we knew that the crews digging inward from the sea had worked their way to meet us.

With the tunnel completed, there remained only one more step before the treasure could be put in place, the

121

floodgate removed and the sea let in, and that was to put stones into the tunnel as a precaution against its collapse once the sea water was allowed in. The section of the tunnel from the airshaft to the floodgate was the most arduous. We were forced to inch our way deep into the black, airless tunnel on our knees, pushing our tray of heavy stones uphill in front of us. Because I had, earlier in the summer, collected the stones and stacked them in the clearing above the tunnel, and because our efforts were encouraged by unrelenting whippings, this task was completed in two days.

On the day we finished, we were taken, not to our usual place in the clearing for the night, but instead were led across the wharf platforms to *The Queen's Privateer*. By then rain was spitting in our faces as the first autumn storm darkened the horizon. Judging from the ominousness of the sky, the tunnel had been finished just in time.

Chapter Twenty-Two

While the slaves were battened down in the ship's hold I was chained to my cabin bunk to wait out the storm. I lay on my mattress, giving my exhausted body over to the storm. Nature, which had been quiescent all summer long, would now have her way with us—and with me. For I knew, as I listened to the storm's anger, that the time had come to assemble my father's pump, that I would at last be put to the use my uncle intended. And with my usefulness at an end, I knew my uncle would kill me. It was just a matter of when and where. Would he wait to throw me overboard with the slaves? Or scuttle me with the crew? Or would he kill me as soon as he knew how to work the pump, and bury me on the island? As I lay on my bunk listening to the storm I desperately tried to think of ways I could delay putting the pump together, and I thought up and rejected plan after plan of how I could escape.

For four days the winds roared at gale force, lifting

the sea in gigantic breakers that crashed against the island shore flooding it, then receded sucking rocks backwards in its wake. The rocks rattled and thundered against one another as they rolled back and forth. The ship, its rigging straining, reared and plunged like a wild stallion, tethered against its will.

Eventually the wind subsided and the rain ceased. Though the breakers no longer foamed, the grey sea swelled restlessly around us. The gulls which had weathered the storm dug into sea grasses, returned, swirling and dipping over the waves in their incessant search for food. The heavy rains had passed, although clouds still hung above us, low as the ship's masts. It was time to go back to work, and still I had thought of no way of escape.

I heard shouts as the crew towed the wharf platforms back onto the water and lashed them into place. They had been taken apart and put ashore so they would not be battered to splinters by the force of the waves. I heard the scrape of wood across the deck and a heavy thumping noise. I knew that the crates storing my father's pump were being taken ashore. This fact was confirmed when my uncle appeared at my door in a rain cape, boots and gloves, ready to finish what he had begun.

"Up you get, Robin," he ordered, "at last the time has come for you to do the job you were paid for."

"I won't do it. I won't help you. If my father were here, he wouldn't either. You're nothing but a filthy pirate, a dishonourable . . ."

My uncle's gloved hand slammed across my mouth shutting off my words. A trickle of blood ran down my lip. My uncle bent over me, his cruel eyes rivetted to mine.

"You will do as I say. Either you assemble that pump

124

or I will have Mr. Boles whip you to death." He straightened up. "And mark my words, it will be a slow, painful death."

The helplessness of my situation overcame me and I began to cry. My uncle took my tears to mean I would do as I was told. He was right. Resistance was impossible.

"And not only will you put together the pump," he went on, "you will show me how to do it."

During the following days he remained as close to me as my shadow.

The pump was to be assembled on the platform directly above the vault where water had gathered during the storm. The pump could draw water from a depth of twenty feet but worked best from a depth of ten, which was why my father had designed the platforms ten feet apart—so that the pump could be moved either up or down the shaft depending on the depth of the water to be removed.

After the crates containing the pump were lowered into the shaft, Billy Boles came to get me, snapping a wrist lock on my arm. Down we went, ladder by ladder, from platform to platform. I dreaded every step I took. Never had the shaft seemed more gloomy or grave-like. Usually it was an active place, with men and equipment moving up and down. Now, with just my uncle, Billy Boles and myself inside, it was grimly silent and forbidding.

When we reached the platform above the vault, Billy Boles fastened my wrist lock to a chain which was attached to an iron stake driven deep into the hard-packed wall of the shaft. Reluctantly, I prepared to assemble the pump. I worked as slowly as possible. I must confess too that I made the pump seem more complicated than it was. In fact, my father's pump worked on the simple principle that when steam condenses into water, a vacuum is created. But though the principle was simple, the work of assembling and operating the pump was not.

First, I puttied the platform so that the excess water that was poured over the pressure chamber to help create a vacuum could be collected and re-used. While I spread the putty, my uncle had Billy Boles fit together the long pipes that would take the water out of the vault and carry it to the surface, as well as a metal chimney my father had designed to funnel out the smoke which would come from the pump's firebox.

My uncle did not work himself. Rather, he watched me closely, partly to memorize what I was doing and partly to keep a guard on me. He had unlocked my wrist chain so that I could work faster. But I continued to move as slowly as I dared. My uncle watched me with increasing irritation and nervousness.

The pressure chamber was the key part of the pump. It was there that the steam condensed, creating the vacuum which sucked up the water from below and afterwards built up pressure to thrust it to the surface. After I had the firebox beneath the boiler in place, my uncle ordered down baskets of wood and barrels of sea water. I could think of no more delays and I began disheartedly to operate the pump. I took a log from the wood basket, chopped it into fine kindling with an axe, and lit the fire to start the water boiling. Once it boiled enough a head of steam was produced which went into the pressure chamber. I then poured cold water over the chamber so that the steam would condense and a vacuum be created. It was this vacuum that sucked up the water from below, and, providing I controlled the pump by turning the right valves at the right time, the water that was sucked up from below would then be thrust up to the surface by a further build-up of steam. Once the pump got going it worked as fast as I could work the valves. My uncle

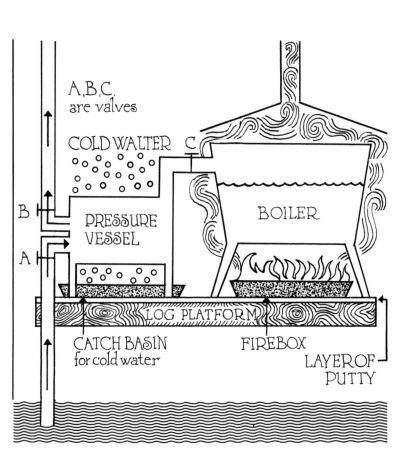

A,B,C.
are valves

COLD WALTER   C

PRESSURE
VESSEL

BOILER

B

A

CATCH BASIN
for cold water

LOG PLATFORM

FIREBOX

LAYER OF
PUTTY

stood directly behind me, watching every move I made. There was a whoosh of water up the pipes as the water was sucked up from below. Then another whoosh and it spurted up the pipes and out of the shaft.

"It works! It works!" my uncle shouted excitedly, marvelling at its success.

Over and over I turned the valves until I became so weary that I stumbled over my own feet. Poor food and back-breaking work had robbed me of my usual stamina. Heat from the fire and lack of air hastened my collapse. My uncle pushed me roughly aside and began to man the pump himself. It was clear he had learned it all by watching me: when to turn the valves, when to pour the cold water over the pressure chamber, when to stoke the fire. I sat on the puttied floor, slumped against the earth wall and watched his long body shadowed in the lantern light.

Another hour's work and the last gurgling suck of water came up the pipe. He was done. His fine clothes were smudged with grime, his shirt soaked with water and sweat but for once he did not seem to notice his appearance—or me.

"At last," he was saying, "at last. Now we put the treasure in place and seal the vault and then no one—not even Satan himself—can find it."

He started up the ladder before he remembered me huddled against the wall.

"You," climbing back down, he kicked my leg, "move off the chain so I can put it on."

Dumbly I moved aside and he snapped the wrist lock back on. Then he was gone, hurrying out of the shaft, moving faster than I had ever seen him move.

He was back within an hour. I heard the wheels of the pulley squeaking far above, Billy Boles' rough voice, my uncle's commands, "Careful now. One at a time. Down.

128

That's good." Then, "I'll go down and unhook them in the vault."

Presently, my uncle swung down the ladder and past me and on into the vault.

Moments later, the first treasure chest, lowered on the pulley hook, came into view, swinging heavily on a rope. It gave me an uncanny feeling, sitting there, watching those treasure chests come down, one by one. There were six of them altogether—each one identical to the other, each one waterproof and airtight.

"All done," I heard Powderlegs high chattering staccato. He could not come down the shaft but was, no doubt, as close to its edge as possible. I heard Billy Boles' heavy boots descending. Down, down, he came, past me and on into the vault below. I could hear his voice mingle eerily with my uncle's, their words rising up through the shaft.

"It's done. I hafta admit I didn't like that pump but it cleared 'er out real good. Yer smart, Cap'n, I'll give you that."

"Why, thank you, Mr. Boles," I heard my uncle say with his usual conceit. "I'm glad we agree. But we're not quite done. We must seal this vault with a thick plug of soil over top and then fill in the shaft with loose soil. After that we pull out the floodgate and then we're done."

"What about the pump? We leave 'er 'ere?"

"No, no, Mr. Boles. We take it apart and keep it with us so we can use it when we return for our chests. Robin will disassemble it and put it in the crates for us."

"That whelp," Billy Boles growled at the mention of my name," 'ee's got to go."

"That's where you're wrong, Mr. Boles. Robin is not going anywhere. He's staying *here*."

"How can 'ee when the shaft's been filled in?"

129

"Come. Come, Mr. Boles. Use your imagination."

"Y' mean, y'bury 'im alive?"

"Not alive, Mr. Boles. Dead. He'll have to be shot. To tidy up before we leave. After all we don't want to leave any loose ends behind us, do we? Since you're so handy with a pistol, you may do it. As soon as he's finished packing the pump, shoot him."

I heard no more, my mind overcome by the certainty of my death. I did not want to die, especially at the hand of Billy Boles.

Chapter Twenty-Three

The next thing I remember I was being kicked in the ribs and Billy Boles was smirking down at me. Now that he knew my death was imminent, he was better disposed toward me.

"Up! 'Ere's the crates. Pack 'em up. Put the pump in 'em. Cap'n says, quick 'bout it."

He stood there until I stumbled wearily to my feet and began the motions of taking the pump apart. I knew if I refused I would be whipped into submission and I did not wish to hasten my death by a painful whipping. When it became obvious to the first mate that with my slow movements it would take me a long time to complete the task, he decided to move on to his own work. He started up the ladder.

"I'll be back. Keep at 'er. Y'know what I'll do if y're not done when I returns," he said ominously and was gone.

Bit by bit I took the pump apart, throwing the parts

carelessly into the crates. The memory of my father's hands, carefully, almost reverently, fitting the parts together came back to me and I began to cry. What a bitter end to his work.

I was down to the last bit of pipe when I heard footsteps coming towards me. I was certain it was Billy Boles, here to fetch the crates.

So great was my misery that I did not even look up when the footsteps reached my ladder. I was stunned when I heard the voice.

"I come to take you back."

I twisted around. Actaudin! There he was standing in the gloom, looking exactly as he had the day we met on shore.

"Actaudin!" I whispered. "You shouldn't have come! Billy Boles will be coming down any minute now. He'll kill you!" I was beginning to panic. This was surely the end. And Actaudin would die too . . . for nothing.

Actaudin shook his head. "No. I leave now. And you come with me."

"But I am chained!"

"I cut you free," he said. He took the axe from the woodpile and pounded the chain with it. Yet even his determination was not enough; trying to cut the iron chain was a hopeless task.

"It won't work," I cried, "the axe cannot cut iron."

This fact quickly became obvious to Actaudin.

"Only one thing to do," he said.

I looked down at the iron band tightly encircling my wrist. I knew exactly what he meant. Between my life and my death was a hand. My hand. If my hand were cut off, the wrist lock would slip off and I would be free.

"I do it fast," Actaudin said. "Take you to Malwalbe. He make good medicine for you."

I had no choice. If I stayed where I was, I would be

132

shot. Yet exchanging my hand for my freedom was a terrible sacrifice. For a few moments I stood there, terrified, unable to make the dreadful move.

Actaudin gave me these moments to gather my courage. Then he said, "We wait no more. We do it fast, before they come."

I stretched out my arm, putting my hand on a slab of wood and closed my eyes. Actaudin raised the axe. Just as he lowered it, I instinctively pulled my arm away and the axe caught my hand, making an ugly slash mark across the back. I gasped with the sharp, slicing pain. In an instant Actaudin had pinioned my arm and brought the axe down hard on my wrist, severing it with this second blow.

I must have fainted, for the next thing I remember was Actaudin pouring cold water over my face and forcing me to sit up. For a moment I was too dazed to realize what had happened to me but my throbbing wrist soon reminded me. It was a shock to look down and see blood spurting from my arm. If it wasn't checked, I would bleed to death without even getting out of the shaft. Though dazed, I remembered my father telling me about a tourniquet—in fact I had watched him tie up a man's arm once after he had accidentally punctured an artery with a knife.

"Help me take off my shirt," I said to Actaudin.

I began struggling out of the shirt and with his help, got it off. I told Actaudin to rip the shirt and make a tight circle of cloth around my forearm. Then instructing him to use a piece of kindling to twist the cloth around my arm as tightly as possible, we managed to make an effective tourniquet. Of course the blood still dripped from the stump but the flow from the main artery had been stemmed. With the rest of the shirt Actaudin made a sling. He then puttied the wound, and wrapped it all round with coconut fibre to keep the putty in place. When that was done, he held onto my good arm and helped me to struggle to my feet. As I did, I noticed my severed hand lying nearby. I remember thinking giddily how strange it was that my arm was in one place and my hand in another. They were no longer joined. My hand lay in front of me, separate, apart, its bloody stump already congealing into dark red clots, its back scarred by an ugly slash mark, its fingers grotesquely clenched into the tight fist I had made. Beside it was the empty iron band.

Before he pulled me up the ladder, Actaudin rolled the hand to the edge of the platform, then kicked it angrily. I remember hearing the thud as it fell down the shaft into the vault below.

Chapter Twenty-Four

Somehow, with Actaudin pulling me by my good arm, we struggled out of the shaft, ladder by ladder, until we reached the top. Actaudin looked about cautiously and when he was assured that the clearing was empty, he helped me up the last few rungs. We dashed across the clearing and into the woods. But not in time. Billy Boles crested the top of the incline at the precise moment we disappeared into the woods. There was a wild yell as he came running into the bushes behind us. Fortunately a shield of drizzling mist hung close to the ground, keeping a protective screen between us and him. Yet we knew we were leaving a trail of broken bushes and blood that he would not find difficult to follow. Though the tourniquet had effectively cut off the arteries, my clothes were covered with blood which smeared onto the leaves as we passed. At first, with Actaudin pulling me forward and my fear urging me on, we were able to keep a fairly steady pace toward the channel. Actaudin did not steer a straight course toward the mainland but zigzagged a roundabout path around the trees in an effort to throw Billy Boles off the trail.

But the first mate was not to be deterred. He was like a fierce mastiff who never tires and never gives up the chase but relentlessly pursues his quarry to the very end. When we at last reached the channel and rushed into the water, we were sure Billy Boles would not follow us into the wilderness on the mainland. But he didn't hesitate. We were halfway across the channel when he waded into the water, holding his pistols high above his head. Gulping down sea water in my panic to make myself move faster, I kicked my legs furiously until I reached shallow water and struck bottom. Actaudin again took hold of my good arm and dragged me into the bushes. The exertion of the swim had weakened me, my arm had begun to bleed again and I began to stagger. I was having difficulty breathing.

"You go ahead," I gasped, "he's after me, not you."

But Actaudin never wavered. If he was tempted to leave me then, he did not show it but only urged me on more strenuously. We were going through a thick stand of fir and had to run crouched-over to avoid the low scratching branches.

Billy Boles was across the water now. We heard him crashing heavily over fallen logs and through underbrush as he kept on our trail. He was gaining on us. He knew it was just a matter of time before I collapsed. Then all he need do was point a pistol at my head and finish me off.

My knees began to wobble badly and my heart thumped wildly in my chest.

"You go ahead," I gasped again, "leave me."

Actaudin said nothing but jerked me harder. I was stumbling badly, slowing him down. Soon both of us

would be victims. Billy Boles was now so close that if one of us fell he would be within firing range. I knew that any minute now my knees would give way beneath me.

It was just at this point, when defeat seemed inevitable, that a clearing in the woods opened up ahead of us. As we burst into the opening we beheld the black body of an enormous she-bear Actaudin called Mooin. Whether she was heading straight for us or we toward her or both I do not know but Actaudin did not wait to find out. He knew the bear, though old and ill-tempered, was unlikely to attack us before hibernation when her belly was fat with berry eating. That is, unless she was angered. In the moment she appeared he decided to anger her. It was a desperate act. He raised his stone hatchet and swung it carefully, aiming it so that it hit her tender nose. The old bear snarled furiously and rising up on her hind paws to her full height, she started toward us. Actaudin was ready for her. As she came forward he dodged us to one side around a thick base of a fir tree so that we came up behind her in a movement so swift that the she-bear was still moving cumbersomely forward.

At precisely that moment Billy Boles came crashing out of the bushes and collided with her. Standing as she was on her hind paws, her height was much greater than his. One angry claw raked across his eyes, the other across his neck. There was no scream, no yell of agony as the bear's sharp claws ripped into his flesh. Perhaps he tried and could not utter a sound. He did manage to thrust his pistols against her and fire. The huge black body shuddered and fell to the ground, knocking the first mate over. He staggered to his feet. Blood poured from his eyes and throat. He groped for a pistol, trying to pull one from beneath the bear's massive body but she was too heavy for even him to budge. Clutching his badly mauled head, Billy Boles sank back onto the ground.

During the first mate's struggle with the bear Actaudin and I had halted our flight. Until I rested and we tightened the tourniquet that had loosened in our flight, it was impossible for me to continue. As soon as we saw Billy Boles' bleeding eyes, his face and throat half torn away, we knew that he could not see. The bear had blinded him. Nor could he speak. Silently we watched him struggle to his feet and lurch from tree to tree in the direction of the water. It was the last I saw of him, or indeed, anyone else aboard *The Queen's Privateer*.

After Billy Boles had left us, I watched Actaudin go to where Mooin lay. For what seemed a long while he stood looking down at the dead bear. Then he stooped down and cut a yellowed tooth from the bear's mouth. This he carefully placed in the pouch at his waist. Later, when we reached his village, he made a thong for the tooth and wore it about his neck as a sign that he had become a man and Mooin his totem.

Chapter Twenty-Five

The years immediately following that fateful summer, I lived with the Micmac. Actaudin and I became brothers, spending many of our days together. But he also spent long hours with Alsoosit who had singled him out to become a leader of his people. In choosing Actaudin for leadership, Alsoosit recognized the inevitability of the white man's coming. He wanted someone who would not easily accept the white man's ways.

Eventually, after Alsoosit died, traders and settlers began to populate the coast, cutting down trees and building houses. Actaudin and his people abandoned their summer camp beside the sea and settled permanently inland at Lake Kedjimkojik. There they avoided much of the bloody struggle which followed the white man's coming as England and France wrestled for control of his land. Actaudin never returned to the island, nor did I, though I lived with the Micmac for almost five years.

Although those years were happy ones for me, I found myself growing restless for England. I wanted to return home before my grandfather died: I hoped he was still alive. Actaudin, respecting my restlessness, encouraged my return, even supplying me with guides and provisions for my journey through the coastal wilderness. Eventually I made my way here to Boston to book passage for home. Having no money, I first had to earn my fare. I was given a job clerking on the waterfront, checking off stores as they were unloaded: barrels of molasses, sacks of sugar, bolts of cloth and kegs of spices— merchant ships from all over the world traded at this thriving port.

It wasn't entirely by coincidence then that I learned the fate of *The Queen's Privateer*. While waiting for the ships to dock, I used to talk to an old sailor whose health, though not his heart, kept him ashore. He loved to spin yarns of the sea, of ships and sailors, storms and shipwrecks. One day he told me the story of how *The Queen's Privateer* had gone down five years before off Sable Island, that watery burial ground of countless ships. It had been during a violent autumn storm: there had been two in a row that year, he said. Everything on the ship was lost—captain, crew, log-books, everything, except a red-haired giant of a man, half-dead, who was picked up by a fishing schooner headed for Boston, a man who could neither read nor write, speak nor see.

On hearing this I began to tremble, as the memories of that dreadful summer flooded my mind.

"He used to sit over there," the old sailor continued, "makin' a fool of himself, reachin' out to passerbys as if he had somethin' to say. Over and over he'd do this. If he got hold of anyone, he'd point seaward and draw the strangest pictures in the sand with a stick. No one paid the slightest attention: we put him down as crazy."

141

And a good thing too, I thought.

"One day I came down here and found him floatin' face down in the water at the end of the wharf. Shot himself, he did, right through the head. After that I got to thinkin' that maybe he wasn't crazy after all. Maybe he was tryin' to tell us somethin' all those years, that he got so frustrated because he couldn't make us understand." The old sailor paused reflectively, looking at the sea whose mystery a lifetime could not fathom. "Whatever it was, it sure must've been somethin' mighty worth the tellin'."

Postscript

Although *The Hand of Robin Squires* is fiction, it is based upon historical facts.

By 1750 the mainland of Acadie on which part of this story takes place was known as Nova Scotia. All along the coast new settlements, notably Halifax, Dartmouth, and Lunenburg, sprang into existence as the tide of new colonists from Europe swept into North America. The particular bay in the story, with its 364 islands, became known as Mahone Bay. Mahone takes it name from the French word *mahonne* meaning a low-lying pirate ship similar to those which frequented the coast in the seventeenth and eighteenth centuries. And the small "S"-shaped island on which this story takes place became known as Oak Island because of the numerous oak trees that grew there.

The search for treasure on Oak Island began in 1795 when three young men: John Smith, Daniel McGinnis and Anthony Smith (aged twenty, sixteen and thirteen respectively) were exploring the island and discovered a depression in the ground beneath an ancient oak tree. An old tackle block was suspended from a branch over-hanging the spot. The three began digging. Ten feet down they came to a log platform. The earth covering the logs was loose yet the sides of the large hole were hard and firm. Twenty feet down they encountered a second platform and at thirty feet a third.

They went no deeper and it was not until 1804 that searchers discovered that the wooden platforms con-tinued every ten feet to the ninety-foot depth and that some of them were covered with what was thought to be coconut fibre and others with putty. At the ninety-foot level, when searchers were confident they were close to the treasure, disaster struck and the pit filled with sixty feet of sea water.

Since that time the excavated shaft has come to be known as "The Money Pit." Companies have been formed to probe the island for its secret which people are certain lies somewhere within its flooded depths. In terms of both human lives and money, the search for treasure on Oak Island has become the most expensive treasure hunt in history. Well over a million dollars has been spent trying to solve its mystery. Four men have lost their lives in an attempt to reach the treasure. Ex-plorations have indicated the presence of tunnelling, of beach-box drains and of triangular stone markers. One drill is said to have passed through "money and pieces," and in 1897 a drill recovered a piece of parchment. Nu-merous shafts have been sunk in and around The Money Pit. To this date no treasure has been found. Still the search continues.

Today the Triton Alliance Company is working on Oak Island. On November 23, 1971, the Company announced to the press that a submarine camera had been lowered into the shaft. It was reported in the *Halifax Chronicle-Herald* that:

A series of pictures show faint outlines of what project manager Dan Blankenship says he is certain are three chests, one having a handle on the end and a curved top. Beside another of the chests or boxes, he says, is some sort of tool, not unlike a pick-axe.

A more gruesome revelation by the camera probing the same cell was the appearance on the monitor of a human hand, partly clenched, suspended in water, Mr. Blankenship said.

Startled by what he saw, Mr. Blankenship said he summoned all his workers, one by one, into the shack housing the television monitor. Each man confirmed that the hand, still covered with flesh, had what looked like a slash mark across the back, while below the mark the mangled flesh suggested it had been torn or chopped from the wrist, he said.

Blankenship told the reporter that he had sought the advice of experts who told him that under certain conditions it would be possible for human flesh to be preserved, especially if it had been imbedded in clay, such as is found at great depths on Oak Island. . . .